John Vance Cheney

Wood Blooms

John Vance Cheney

Wood Blooms

ISBN/EAN: 9783744641081

Printed in Europe, USA, Canada, Australia, Japan

Cover: Foto ©Andreas Hilbeck / pixelio.de

More available books at **www.hansebooks.com**

WOOD BLOOMS

BY

JOHN VANCE CHENEY

Author of "Thistle-Drift"

NEW YORK

FREDERICK A. STOKES & BROTHER

MDCCCLXXXVIII

TO
MY FATHER

THE SINGER OF TO-DAY.

*M*UCH *as Calisto stood before*
     Diana's maids, the time she was
Heavy with child of Jupiter,
Stands Genius, great with thought, before
The reproving world. Whoso, indeed,
Dare not declare the gift from Heaven,
Must blush with a fair shame; confused,
Must bring his little light as one
That bears a candle to the air
In the scant hollow of his hand.
Doubt follows like a shadow, faith
Does shake, troubles beset the way;
And yet the son of song, true born,
Holds onward. What he is, he is;
And nurslings of a lesser breed

Cannot undo his birth, nor end
His work.   The harvest may be light,
But what is reaped will wear the gold :
This is enough.   Nor let them chide,
His brawny brothers, called to put
The sickle in a fuller field :
Forsooth, stronger than they as they
Than he, have been.   The ground is old ;
Ay, what is left for any, now ?
Simply to fitly echo—pass
The great First Voices down the years.
Exceeding few may be far heard—
Too true ; still it is a brave reach
To sweetly take the nearest heart.

CONTENTS.

	PAGE
Hilda	I
St. Isophore	3
Old Braddock	7
The Revenge	12
The Three Ages	16
Hokan, the Hermit	24
The House of Pleasure	26
The White Tower	32
Then	34
Apart	36
A Day Dream	37
On the Wild Ways of the Night . . .	39
Night Wind of Fall (I.)	40
" " (II.)	40

	PAGE
Song of the Sea	42
The Voice	43
Insane	44
The Shadow	46
The Shape Unseen	47
Back of it all is Fate	48
Bleeding Heart and Broken Wings . .	49
Dirge	50
Dear Maid, pale as the pale Wild Dove .	51
Voice of the Past	52
Memory	53
Calm	54
The Strong	56
The Dead Hero (I.)	57
" " (II.)	57
To the Bitter End	59
He that Hears the Voice	61
Faith	63
At Last	64

PAGE

The Use of Sorrow 66

Rest upon the Hill. 67

The Glories of Two Worlds 68

My Children 69

My Dreams 70

A Wish 72

My Choice 73

My Castle in the Air 74

Deep within the Forest Gray . . . 75

In Twilight Land 76

Waiting 78

The Old 80

Our Mother 81

The Heart's Sovereignty 82

Death's 83

The Guest 84

The Confession 91

Who's for the Magdalen? 97

The Empty Arbor 101

	PAGE
The Wind	104
Song and Silence	106
The Trees	107
Spring Song (1) (My thoughts—they swing;)	108
" " (2) (Now back again to brown, etc.)	108
" " (3) (The maple and the birch, etc.)	109
Morning Song in Summer	111
Summer Hours	113
The Brook	115
Summer Noon	117
August Days	118
The Stranger-Days	120
Going of Autumn	121
Death of Autumn	123
November	126
Fancy's Flock	127
On the Upper Ways	129
The Poet	132
The Pilgrimage	134

		PAGE
The Sacred Veil	. . . . . .	136
Toung Taloung	. . . . .	139
The Silent Blessing	. . . .	142
In the Lane	. . . . . .	145
Good By (Song)	. . . . .	148
By and By (Song)	. . . . .	149
What's in this Christmas Day?	. . .	151
Great is To-day	. . . . .	157
Every one to his own Way	. . . .	159
The Good Old-time	. . . .	161
Granther	. . . .	164
A Saint of Yore	. . . . .	167
The Old Farm Barn	. . . .	170
Auto da fé	. . . . . .	173
An Epistle to a Bachelor	. . . .	179
Brother Bachelor Batrachian	. . .	184
Our Ophidian Friend	. . . .	189
Silver Bell	. . . . . .	192
Helen	. . . .	201

	PAGE
Poetry made Practic	209
The Trapper's Sweetheart	213
The Jockey's Soliloquy	215
Modern Progress	218

HILDA.

GRAY Hilda to the churchyard came,
    A withered gypsy, bent and lame ;
Straightway she struck her witches' light—
Three greenish flames, sharp-tongued and bright.

Next, she the magic circle drew,
Caught thrice three leaves the night wind blew ;
Then fixèd, as in death, sat she
Among the graves all silently.

So sat she till the village clock
Struck twelve ; with its last, warning shock
She broke the charm—sent back below
The dim shapes gliding to and fro.

These passed, but till the darkness fled
Old Hilda sat among the dead ;
Where, overhead, night long a bough
Did sigh, and since has sighed till now.

At morn she rose, cried thrice aloud,
"Young Winsted, when she wears her shroud,
The fish shall feed !"   Then, thin and gray,
Like a live mist, she went her way.—

God rest her soul—old Hilda gray !
The dreary morn they laid away
The maid beneath the churchyard tree
Curst Winsted's ship went down at sea.

ST. ISOPHORE.

WHO now serves the Master,
  Heals the sick from door to door,
As did he—God-fearing,
  Faithful, brave Saint Isophore?

"Healer, heal thy thousand,"
  —Plain he heard the voice divine—
" Lives a thousand, save them ;
  One thereafter—forfeits thine."

All but to the limit,
  Firm he wrought his round two-score ;
Then the voice of warning,—
  Dost forget, good Isophore ?

Thoughtful, faintly smiling,
  " I remember well," he said ;
" But one more—one only,
  And I number with the dead."

Calm he sat and questioned,
  Took still counsel with his heart,
Whether it were better
  He should tarry or depart.

Nature—well he loved her,
  Loved the forest and the field ;
  These were lost forever
If again he touched and healed.—

Now the king was stricken,
  Isophore they sought to bring ;
" Nay," he answered, " life is
  Sweet to beggar as to king."

Fathers, mothers, children,
Rich and poor, and young and old
Gathered to the healer ;
" Nay," he said, " the scroll is rolled."

But, ere long one entered,
Beautiful as flesh may be ;
At his feet she threw her—
" Man of God, Oh, pity me !

" Faithful have I promised
One that lives beyond the sea ;
He is coming, father,
And I die.   Oh, pity me ! "

Filled with fear and anguish,
Looked she in the healer's face ;
Like a marble statue,
Sat he, silent, in his place.

White he sat, and silent,
    Thinking backward on the years ;
Sudden to the maiden
    Turned he, smiling, but in tears,—

" Daughter, little dreaming
    What thou askest, why I give,
Get thee to thy lover,
    To thy—mother ; go, and live !"

Merry was the wedding ;
    So the bride shone years before,
When was wed the mother,
    Faithless to young Isophore.

Merry was the wedding
    While the good ship stood off shore ;
At that hour the spirit
    Passed from peerless Isophore.

OLD BRADDOCK.

FIRE ! Fire in Allentown !
The Women's Building—it must go.
Mothers wild rush up and down,
Despairing men push to and fro ;
Two stories caught—one story more—
See—see—old Braddock 's to the fore,
Braddock, full three-score.

Like a high granite rock
His good gray head looms huge and bare ;
Firm as rock in tempest shock
He towers above the tallest, there.
" Conrad ! " 'Tis Braddock to his son,
The prop he thinks to lean upon
When his work is done.

Conrad, the young and brave,
Unflinching meets his father's eye :
" Who would now the children save,
That they die not himself must die."
On his white face no touch of fear,
But, O, it is so sweet, so dear—
Life at twenty year !

" Father—Father ! " A quick
Embrace, and he has set his feet
On the ladder.   Rolling thick,
The flame-shot smoke chokes all the street,
So blinds one only has descried
Her form that, thro' its dreadful tide,
Springs to Conrad's side.

Strong she is, now, as he,
Throbbing with love's own lion might ;
Strong as beautiful is she,
And Conrad's arms are pinioned tight.

" Far thro' the fire, sits God above "—
In vain he pleads ; full does it prove,
Her full strength of love.

Too late she sets him free—
High overhead his father's call :
From a height no eye can see
Calls hoary Braddock down the wall,—
" Old men are Death's, let him destroy,
Young men are Life's, Conrad, my boy—
Life's and Love's, my boy ! "

Wilder the women's cries,
Hoarser the shouts of men below ;
Sheets of fire against the skies,
Set all the stricken town aglow.
With sweep and shriek, with rush and roar,
The flames shut round old Braddock hoar—
Braddock, full three-score.

" Save, save my children, save ! "

" Ay, ay,' all answer, speak as one,

" If man's arm can from the grave

    Bring back your babes, it will be done ;

    Know Braddock still is worth us all—

    Hark—hark !   It is his own brave call,—

' Back—back from the wall ! ' "

God ! God, that it should be !

As savagely the lashed wind veers,

Fiercer than the fiery sea

The frantic crowd waves hands, and cheers ;

An old man high in whirl of Hell !

The children—how, no soul can tell—

Braddock holds them well.

Shorn all that good gray head

With snows of sixty winters sown ;

Griped around the children's bed,

One arm is shriveled to the bone :

" Old men are Death's, let him destroy.

Young men are Life's, Conrad, my boy,

Life's and Love's, my boy ! "——

Fire ! Fire in Allentown !

Though 'twas a hundred years ago,

How the babes were carried down,

To-day the village children know.

They know of Braddock's good gray head,

They know the last, great words he said,

Know how he fell—dead.

THE REVENGE.

THE struggling stars dim light
　　The palace wall and pane ;
Why chafes the dog, to-night,
　　In bondage of his chain ?

He sees a pallid face
　　And spectral eyes that stare;
Quicker his restless pace,
　　Stiffer stands his hair.

Dear face ! he knows it well,
　　Knows, too, that vapor hand ;
He gives a grin of Hell,
　　He tries his brazen band.

Again—once more ; he 's free !
  The spectre beckons on,
And, swift as sight may be,
  Both ghost and dog are gone.

It is a trackless way
  Across the lowland hoar,
But, oh, the spectre gray
  Has traveled it before !

The clock has struck but twice
  Since she was in her tower ;
And when it shall strike thrice,
  'Twill be the midnight hour.

She heard a voice below
  Was like her lover's call ;
Soft thither did she go,
  She passed the palace wall.

Down like a dove she flew,
    All soft she fluttered down :
Cunning the craven drew
    The gentle lady down.

God blot, blot out his sin
    That lured the lady down—
The moon is old and thin
    In wilds beyond the town.

He's hid her body there,
    The flesh is not yet cold :
" Let lady fair beware
    That frowns on suitor bold !

" Go, tell thy high-born folk
    Whose quiet bride thou art "——
Never more he spoke ;
    The dog did lap his heart.——

The cleared stars fling their light
  On palace wall and pane :
What glistens there so bright ?
  It is the empty chain.

THE THREE AGES.

I.

CHEERLY greet me—I am young !
   Never blithest poet sung
Of one that happier found his way
To golden gladness of the day :
With music meet me, play and sing
To give me merry welcoming !

Life is fair, and love is sweet ;
Hardly may you see my feet,
So airy light, so fleet I come,
Henceforth to make the world my home.
Strew flowers, lift the ringing voice,
Sing songs with me—rejoice, rejoice !

Glad is youth, joyous and strong !
Time has sworn to do no wrong ;
I take your hand—come, let us run
With laughter in the open sun !
Feel how I clasp you, hold you fast ;
For life is kind, and love will last.

Nay, shake not the doubtful head,
Withered Sorrow—he is dead ;
Young Joy has buried him so deep
Never again shall mourner weep.
Yes, life is kind, will grow more dear
From day to day, from year to year.

Gaily greet me—viols, play ;
Hours, go dancing down the day,
And I will with you laughing run
Like meadow-brook at rise of sun.
Ho, all come follow ; sorrow 's past,
And life is sweet, and love will last !

II.

Whither art faring ? Is one half
The road-room not enough ? You laugh ;
'Tis a loon's answer. Do not stop,
Be off ! Ay, spin it like a top
The way they go that chase a smile ;
Till night is but a little while,
And Fool-town 's east good twenty mile.

Twice I 've bid you be gone. You heard ;
But heavens ! a callow, limp-necked bird
Just out the shell, all belly, beak—
Once more I 'll have compassion. Speak,
Then—briefly ; Time, though old, is fast
And tireless.—" Sorrow, it is past,
And life is sweet, and love will last."—

Enough. You 've yet hard hills to climb.
Your mother wasted nine months' time

Out of the twelve, the year she bore
A son.   One word—you 'll wish no more—:
Play bubbles, blow, puff out of breath,
Hug life, swallow each word she saith—
Boy, did you ever hear of *death ?*——

I thought it—gone.   That last hard word
Pricked in the crop of my young bird.
How gay he skims it on to town !
The jaunty twitching of his gown,
His curvets—truly that is grace ;
And his as plump, ungrooved a face
As any's of the Fool-town race.

With savage thrust I shoved him by,
But such as he is, that was I :
All smirks and nods, and faith sublime
In every cruel trick that time
Did play me.   Forty year at school,

I measure with too ready rule—
Ah, well, peace to the pretty fool.

III.

The sun is low, once more he nears his rest,
And dark, dulling the purple of the west,
Prepares the way of night.   Upon the hill
The night-wind, loosed, now wanders at its will,
With moaning.   The clear call at break of day
ᛁEchos, a sigh, when night has passed away :
The dawn, the noon, then gloom upon the gold,
And music fallen a-wailing.   I am old ;
Nature misleads me not as in my youth,
She pities me my years, and speaks the truth—
Wise mother, tend'rest when the leaping heart
Is slowed, and Joy has played her careless part.—
The wind is louder ; like a beast it growls,
Or, sweeping down the gorges, fitful howls ;

The windows shudder, while the taller trees
Whip wildly in the wood : I take mine ease.—
Old winds, roar on !   I am as grim and hoar
As are your eldest ; barred mine oaken door,
Ay, steel of years is barred across my breast :
Old winds, ye cannot touch an old man's rest.—
Serene his spirit, steady is his head
That travels best the highway toward the dead.
To make this sober journey are we sent ;
If, chance, a momentary ornament
We be besides, 'tis but a fire-fly's glow,
A flash, which does not light the way we go.
For this, and only this, lives every one :
Calmly to work, to rest when work is done.
To-day, a youth passed by, singing along
The highway ; merry as a brook's his song ;
Where, caroling, he hastened into sight,
There shone a glistening mirror of delight :
So fair his face, so tuneful, smooth, his tongue,
I know not if he sweeter looked or sung.

So did he look and sing, thoughtless and gay,
To-morrow to be sad as glad, to-day.
There met him as he, laughing, leapt and ran,
One come to middle years, a dark-browed man :
Matching his frown against the weanling's smiles,
With dagger words he stabbed at fortune's wiles
As they were bodies to be whittled down.
This man, years since, did win him high re-
    nown
As fame goes ; having won, he sudden paused,
Disowned his honors, saying they had caused
But loss.   Angered he rose, without delay
Forever from old follies turned away—
Away from olden follies unto new ;
For rage holds not the golden balance true.—

But why, forsooth, sit I and muse on these ?
Impossible to share with them mine ease.
Indifferent, too, are old men, though we feel
Somewhat as into shadow slow we steal.

Age *is* indifferent : in the eyes of Thought

There be few tears, his tightened lips smile not.

And yet, O Youth, all laughter—Man, all war,

These white hairs, they must ask, What for—What

    for ?

HOKAN, THE HERMIT.

I HAVE not dwelt with men, but have held close
   Unto thy breast ; Mother, remember this.
The earth is gray, and yonder climbing sun
Is old, but both keep yet the youthful green
And the young gold.   These are my rightful kin ;
Why me, why cut me off and touch them not ?
If time's insidious chiseling mark my cheek,
If flood of years wash white these hairs—to die
For that !   I say, I have not lived with men,
Why die with them?   Surely my shoulders hold
As they were set, unbent by packèd care ;
I walk upright, my sleep is long and sound,
Rest lays her thighs to mine in my still bed.
Only dead hope should rot.   Wait till I wail

For woe that flattens me like a great stone,

Bear with me till I rail against my lot,

Till first I whine.   You take not yon gray rock :

He, too, is old.   Mother, remember me.

Strike down the sapless oak, the spineless grass

Which withers ; ay, lick up the trickling stream,—

But shall the sea be dried, wilt stop the stars ?

Older are these, older than I, and less ;

Take them or take not me.   Th' Etruscan king

Did bind the living hand to hand, and face

To face, fast to the dead, there let them die.

You will not so.   Mother, you are not hard,

Like kings, and I am not as other men.

Last night the moon did stop on yonder hill,

Did pause and gaze as one that looks her last

On the beloved : Mother, remember me.

THE HOUSE OF PLEASURE.

THE sun burns not with purer gold
    Than flamed that palace famed of old :
Proudest of all the gorgeous piles of slumber,
Around me shot its columns tall ;
Glory poured over floor and wall
Thick, dazing splendors without name or number.

Anon, rich singing rose and fell :
" O youth," it ran, " we love thee well,
We love thee well !" And I could feel their
    breathing,
So near the singing maidens drew—
The wingèd maidens, as they flew,
Singing, dancing, their arms like wild vines wreath-
    ing.

Once, when the rapturous song ran low,

One pressed me to her breast, aglow,

Whereon I sank, bewildered, dizzy clinging :

My face pressed hard its pillow warm,

While still swept on the blended storm

Of light and laughter, of dancing and of singing.

O, long and long there did I lie,

Until the day did fade and die ;

And when I woke, fled was the rapturous measure,

Not one sweet voice, not one lithe form ;

No more the live breast, soft and warm,

But cold dead stone—the throne of the House of
      Pleasure.

The throne it was, for through the night,

I read in letters burning bright,

Like low stars in the pine-tops,—*Thou beholdest*

The king of the Realm of Pleasure—the king,

High lord of youth and reveling,
Sovereign of sovereigns from gray years the oldest.

"Dread shape," I sighed, "art thou the king ;
To thee, at last, does Beauty bring
Her sons of mirth, her daughters dancing, singing?"
Behold the King of Joy ! he said.
Lo, there were no eyes in his head,
And round him vapors of the vault were clinging—

Vapors that made a dreadful veil,
And, as the light seeds start and sail
Along the summer wind, shape followed shape
About in it : with gesture slow
The king did sign, and they did go,
And a serpent looped, and swung from the king's
      nape.

" 'Fore God," I cried, " thou king of bone,
Canst call this temple—all—thine own?"

How old art thou? he asked ; and the serpent
　　turning,
Reared its slim head as if to hear.
I answered, " Record me twenty year."—
'*Tis done : behold the record, yonder, burning.*

On the cold white steps, facing the throne,
I lay before the king of bone,
And counted the twenty tapers faintly burning :
Fixed in a glass of slipping sand,
Twenty pale shapes had them in the hand,
Who a noiseless march slow round and round 'gan
　　turning.

The first shape in his misty hand
Held up the taper, set in sand,
Whereat the king signed the sign there is no denying :
Upheld, I watched it prick the air,
I saw it drop to the sand, and flare,
And it was smothered ere I knew 'twas dying.

As the first shape came the second came,
And held on high the fated flame—
Again the direful sign there is no denying:
The chilling, dim-lit stone was wet   .
As with the drench of the last sweat,
Where I stared, dumb, before the monarch lying.

Noiseless, the filmy shapes filed on
Till, all save one, the flames were gone:
A moment more—the final sign would be given,
But one more wave of the fleshless hand,
And the last would sink to the slipping sand,
And my soul go forth and be as the leaf wind-driven.

I clutched at the cold glazed stone, and cried,—
" Now, monstrous king, art thou defied,
Scorned in her name whose I am from the morrow!"
I spoke her name, and, as I spoke,
In the ghastly place a great light broke,

And in the midst stood, bowed, the dark queen,
   Sorrow.

I clung to her black robe, and prayed,—
" Let yon sand slip not, bid the flame be stayed ! "
The sand slackened, and to a mournful measure
The flame spread bright and wide till, at last,
His pale train sank, and the crowned skull passed,
And the dropt snake writhed on the site of the
   House of Pleasure.

THE WHITE TOWER.

BUILT in my dreams, a white tower rose,
    And she that was its light stood at the door
The beams of moon and star fell pale around her,
The four winds silent gathered.

Ere long, slow floated tones far-borne,
As of a voice had wandered out of Heaven,
Burdened with melody no ear could reach to,
Only for spirits' hearing.

Even as it came the wide air curled
Upon itself till, like a mighty shell,
Trembling, it swung and sweetly murmured—mur-
        mured,
Filled with immortal music.

Full in the white-tower door stood she
About whose feet the beams of moon and star
Fell wan as ashes ; motionless, unheeding,
She stood, as it were, the statue

Of some stopt soul held fast between
The seen and the unseen—a spirit clothed
In radiant semblance of its mortal vesture,
Midway 'twixt earth and Heaven.

Now sped, swift as the hunter's shaft,
A cry from earth, her lover's cry of pain
Sent up from loss unutterable—last anguish
Of a great heart, so broken.—

Still stood, unchanged, the high white tower,
But in the door no more the shape of flame :
A track of fire ran from it, burning earthward—
Spake Heaven, *They come together.*

THEN.

NOT yet, O Love ! not yet.
 Till from high brightness of the past
Not one sole beam of splendor last,
Lift not thine eyes to mine,
Take not my hand in thine.
  O Love ! not yet—
   Not yet.

Not yet, O Love ! not yet.
Till in the future thou canst see,
In soulless thing or soul, but me,
Bid not my held heart break
Its fetters for thy sake.
  O Love ! not yet—
   Not yet.

Not yet, O Love ! not yet.
Till the full present shut thee round,
Wall in thy soul from sight and sound
Between thy heart and me,
I must not follow thee.
O Love ! not yet—
Not yet.

But when this is, Oh, then,
Though 'twixt us stretch the mighty sea,
Thine arms will feel they 're folding me !
Thy heart emptied, swept clean
As though love had not been,
My love, Oh, then—
Then, Then !

APART.

APART—too hard that word to say.
    'Twere death to me to take away
What I do love ; myself were taken.
Never was love like mine forsaken :
When thou art gone, 'twill be too late
For me to feel my fate.

Thou going, I shall going be,
O Love ! beyond the loss of thee ;
Thou gone, I 'll not be left to grieve :
Love cannot true love living leave.
Apart—to me 'twere idly said ;
They hear not that are dead.

A DAY DREAM.

'TWAS not 'neath spectral moon,
But in the day's high noon,
That, pillowed on the grass,
I saw a vision pass.

Strange quiet folded round,
Strange silence, close—profound ;
Sweet peace, peace sweet and deep,
Bade every trouble sleep.

"O Spirit ! stay with me,
Lying all quietly :
If this is death," I said,
" Be my lot with the dead."

The shape with others passed,

Each fainter than the last ;

And—dreadful was the roar—

I heard the day once more.

ON THE WILD WAYS OF THE NIGHT.

ALAS, who did it, Fall wind, sighing ;
  Who struck her cheek so white
That she walks there—glides, a-dying,
  On the wild ways of the night?

Night wind, no longer let her wander ;
  Poor ghost, that she should freeze !
Call her, bid her over yonder
  To the shelter of the trees.

The bitter, oh, th' unpitying weather !
  Ere moon and stars be dead,
Blow the yellow leaves together,
  Night wind, make the maid a bed.

NIGHT WIND OF FALL.

I.

TO-NIGHT, the might of the wind !
  Let him listen that dare :
Hark—hark—the cry i' the mind,
  Like the wail in the branches bare !

Each thought upcaught by the gale,
  Torn from memory's mold,
The heart's dead wander and wail
  With the flying leaves, a-cold.

II.

Hear the bare boughs sigh
As the winds go by :

Never more hopeless moan,—
Lone, so lone ! "

See, the folding cloud
Is the dead moon's shroud :
Over and over the moan,—
" Lone, so lone ! "

SONG OF THE SEA.

BLACK is the night, the shore lights glare,
  The cries at the hearthside—what is the prayer?
'Tis wind and darkness, tears and moan,
'Tis waiting and wail on the shore, alone :

  God be
  With the ships at sea !

Round the rock-lights and down the bay,
Why comes the wild wind, ay, what does he say ?
He comes to mourn with the souls on shore,
For those that will follow the waters no more :

  Wail, wail
  For the ships that sail !

THE VOICE.

NO birds sing,
    Tranced the air ;
The lattice vines close cling,
    Close keeps the shadow there.

Shade by shade,
    Drifts of gray
Slow dull the footprints made
    Where passed the golden day.

Earth and sky,
    Deep their rest—
Was that the wind went by,
    Or a soul, escaped the breast ?

INSANE.

MY darling hopes went sailing on a summer sea,
    Went sailing, happy sailing, far away from
      me :
All in a shining boat, away—away—from me,
Far did my dear ones float along the summer sea.

O, then this hair was brown ; O, then this face was
    fair !
The boat danced up and down like a leaf upon the
    air.
And bright was then my eye—there could no bright-
    er be ;
I saw the black fiend fly, a-scowling on the sea.

White as this hair is white, the white foam came
    ashore ;

The boat passed out of sight, I heard the storm-beast
    roar :

White as this hair is white, the white foam came
    ashore,

The black fiend laughed outright—my darlings come
    no more.

THE SHADOW.

HELEN, you once were young; with viny grace
　　Enwreathed, the fairest of your gentle race;
Now, Helen, in yon palace I may see
The prosperous sire, the children at your knee.

Perhaps my sight played false the night—our last·
When in the bright moonshine a spectre passed;
But, Helen, gentle Helen, is it peace,
Do no dreams come, no longings for release?

Helen, our love—went it like summer weather,
The golden dreams and golden days together?
Soft mother, which the shadow, after all,
You or that following on your costly wall?

THE SHAPE UNSEEN.

BESIDE two lovers stands a shape,
 A watchful shape, unseen ;
His ear is at their hearts,
 His hands their hands between.

The sigh, the vow—he heeds not these,
 The heart is all his care ;
The lips that kiss may curse,
 The heart—he hearkens there.

Cry not to him ; as kind as wise,
 He will not idly pain :
The hands he tears apart,
 They should not clasp again.

BACK OF IT ALL IS FATE.

THE son of strength may strike and win,
 Or to the hungry dust go down ;
The full blood flows, and the toils begin,
 To end—God knows—in rags or crown :
  Early and late
  Back of it all is Fate.

Love's high-born daughter—like the rose
 She plucks or passes, so is she ;
To be worn upon the breast—God knows—
 Or under foot trod ruthlessly :
  Early and late
  Back of it all is Fate.

BLEEDING HEART AND BROKEN WINGS.

A BARD, unheard, sang sweetest lay,
   (Our life—it is a little day ;)
The death-glaze made his bright eye dim,
When all the world called after him.

A maiden gave her heart away,
   (Our life—it is a bitter day,)
And there was scandal thro' the town :
Only the bell-toll hushed it down.

The maiden loves, the poet sings,
   (Dear bleeding heart, poor broken wings !)—
Oh, that th' indifferent grave could hear,
The living turn the heedless ear !

DIRGE.

SWEET flower in perfect bloom,
   Thy leaves shall withered be ;
Lone winds above thy tomb,
  Shall nightly sigh with me—
  Sigh with me.

Blithe brook of merry song,
  Thy goal 's the moaning sea ;
Thy laughter spent, ere long
  Thou 'lt mourn, ay, moan with me—
  Moan with me.

All days, with love's short day,
  Steal on to darkness deep :
Beauty shall pass away,
  Nor mirth her measures keep-
  Weep, oh, weep !

DEAR MAID, PALE AS THE PALE WILD DOVE.

DEAR maid, pale as the pale wild dove,
  Wand'ring the silent ways, alone,—
Wide up and down the land of love
  Why made you moan—why made you moan?

My list'ning heart, it ever hears,
  As in the summers long ago:
Shy, sweet wild dove, flown from the years,
  Oh, what strange hurt did grieve you so?

VOICE OF THE PAST.

HAST heard the murmuring *aves* said
 In forest cloister, overhead ;
Hast heard those voices low that fare,
Unpiloted, along the heights of air—

Far melodies too faint for light,
On upper pathways of the night ?
The Past calls in so sweet a tone
These strive and die, nor make it once their own.

MEMORY.

WOULD you Love's fairest daughter see,
　　Yonder she is—sweet Memory :
A statue of unconscious grace,
She stands with bowed, averted face.

CALM.

HAST thou been down into the depths of thought
      Until the things of time and sense are naught;
Hast sunk—sunk—in that tideless under-deep
Fathoms below the little reach of sleep?

Dark, there, and silence; sound is not, nor sun;
The heaving breast, the beating heart, have done:
They lie no stiller whose stopt pulse and breath
Respect the dread repose in realms of death.

Hast visited below, where he must go
That would wisdom's last-yielded secret know?
Hast been a guest where, lost to smiles and tears,
The quiet eye looks on beyond the years?

Hast thou been down into the depths of thought
Until the things of time and sense are naught ?
Then toil and pain blend sweet as evening psalm,
Then doubt is whelmed in hope and care in calm.

THE STRONG.

DOST deem him weak that owns his strength is
   tried?
  Nay, we may safely lean on him that grieves:
The pine has immemorially sighed,
   Th' enduring poplar's are the trembling leaves.

To feel, and bow the head, is not to fear,
   To cheat with jest—that is the coward's art:
Beware the laugh that battles back the tear,
   He's false to all that's traitor to his heart.

He of great deeds does grope amid the throng
   Like him whose steps toward Dagon's temple bore;
There's ever something sad about the strong—
   A look, a moan, like that on ocean's shore.

THE DEAD HERO.

I.

NATURE'S large souls, like the large stars, are
few,
And he was of them ; cloud-crowned Thessaly
Bore not a truer, nobler son than he
That with great need in equal greatness grew,

Grappled with giant wrongs, and overthrew,
Then, in the peaceful days he made to be,—
The war-born third of our immortal three,—
Remembered not the dreadful sword he drew.

II.

In his strength a soldier, in his rest a sage ;
His youth went in war—was it peace in his age?

The dead tell no tales, but a voice in my ears
Says, "Valor belongs to the noiseless years."

Honor to the dead!   A hero is gone.
Hang up his good sword, put his cerements on;
Chance Yonder they know but how he fought
In the thick of peace, in the still of thought.

TO THE BITTER END.

LEST they should mock his woe, he shed no tears,
  Lest they should brand him coward, made no
    moan ;
Mute as themselves, he did endure his years,
  Eating his bread as it were not a stone :
Mute as themselves, he did endure his years

Ambition masked in tame humility
  That yokes for equal draught the ox with man,
None heard him speak again of what might be:
  True to his toil, with neither hope nor plan,
None heard him speak again of what might be.—

Fate, yoked, and goaded by your vassals all,

    You could not wring from him the craven's cry:

Patient as are the cattle of the stall,

    Dumb as the tumbled clods that on him lie,

So patient, dumb, he toiled—so did he fall.

HE THAT HEARS THE VOICE.

THRICE blest is he that hears the voice
    Above belittling strife—
The rolling psalm as they rejoice,
    Th' exultant Sons of Life.

He does not doubt ; he seeth clear,
    And walketh in his trust :
With neither faltering nor fear,
    He meeteth what he must.

To him sorrow is sweet as mirth,
    And toil is one with rest ;
The death groan is the cry at birth,
    The grave the mother breast.

Through veil of darkness wasted thin,
    To him the vision comes :
He sees them that pass out and in
    The high, immortal homes.

FAITH.

NO help in all the stranger-land,
O fainting heart, O failing hand?
There's a morning and a noon,
And the evening cometh soon.

The way is endless, friendless? No;
God sitteth high to see below.
There's a morning and a noon,
And the evening cometh soon.

Look yonder on the purpling West:
Ere long the glory and the rest.
There's a morning and a noon,
And the evening cometh soon.

AT LAST.

DRIFTING slow and aimlessly,
A mist comes on across the sea;
It floats against a sunny hill,
Folds round it, and is still.

Onward—onward, reach by reach,
A great wave shoulders toward the beach;
A mighty rush—it gains the shore,
Nor roves nor moans it more.

Over field and steepled town
A bird goes flying up and down;
Soon comes the friendly twilight hour—
It finds a quiet bower.

Knotted was yon sleeper's brow,

Lo, it is as the snowdrift, now :

Sweeter sleeps care by kind death kissed,

Than bird, or wave, or mist.

THE USE OF SORROW.

NOT from Joy's hand the boons for aye ;
He gives but toys, pleasing, to-day,
To-morrow, willing put away :
Only wise Sorrow holds the heart,
Gives gifts with which we cannot part.
Best friend is Grief.   Believe, believe
It is a blessèd thing to grieve ;
Knowledge and pleasure dwell apart,
Wisdom mates with the broken heart.
Only the eyes cleansed oft with tears
Perceive the meaning of the years :
Unto the sight thus purified,
The gates of mystery open wide ;
And patient watching makes to know
This life and that to which we go.

REST UPON THE HILL.

THE angle, multiplied,
  Does in the circle cease ;
Life's thousand grievances
  Round, by and by, in peace.

The dismal mist below,
  Is radiant cloud above ;
The spirit darkened here,
  Shall shine with heavenly love.

Skyward ascends the stream
  That moves the humble mill ;
We that in valleys toil,
  Shall rest upon the hill.

THE GLORIES OF TWO WORLDS.

THE spirit that delights in visions fair,
  Wherever it may seek, will find them there :
Mountain and valley, woodland, stream and field,
They touch the heart of care—the hurt is healed.

Beauty is nature's Ruth ; close does she cling
Unto her mother, ever following ;
And yet to nature is there never given
One little downward look from eyes of Heaven.

Two glories—not of earth, though deemed her own—
Are gazed upon from splendor of the throne :
We claim two shapes angels lean out to see—
The aged saint, the child upon her knee.

MY CHILDREN.

MY precious buds of flesh and blood,
 That cling about my knee,
I dread the pressing thoughts that dwell
 Upon the years to be.

They say, more kind the early blight
 Than are the ripening suns ;
They say, to blossom is to fall,
 My sweet unfolding ones.

" Only the children's hidden hearts
 Go down, unhurt, to rest " ! —
I tremble at the voice, and hold
 You closer to my breast.

MY DREAMS.

AS I look forward down the years,
   I see less smiling and more tears ;
I see the sunlight slip away,
And shadow wrap the shortened day.
Far, fitfully the hill-top gleams,
Fainter the music of the streams :
O Time ! take them—the music, beams,
But leave my dreams—my dreams.

Old friends, dear ones—I may not say
When they shall tire, and drop away ;
I would not speak for mine own strength,
Nor fix the shadow's growing length.

I ask but that till, one by one,

Life's last flames flicker and—are done,

Thou put not out mine old heart-gleams :

O Time ! take last my dreams.

A WISH.

ONE slowly toils his way to fame,
  And wins, well earned, an envied name;
One vaults into eternity—
Got of the gods, strong-limbed is he.

A few do quench ambition's fire
With ample mantle of the sire;
The thousands ask, when time's no more,
Safe guidance to the Golden Shore.

When my poor self is laid away,
I would the shepherd boy might say,
  —Tuning his pipe less merrily—
" A bough turns sere in Arcady.

MY CHOICE.

I'D rather be
  'Neath a greenwood tree,
With a song and a handful of daisies,
Than the darling of victory
In the blaze of the wide world's praises.

I 'd rather ride
On the wings inside,
Which waft where the world may not after,
Than fold fair Fame as a bride,
To feed on her sighs and her laughter.

MY CASTLE IN THE AIR.

OR in the East or in the West,
    Where shall I build my bird a nest;
Northward or southward—whither roam
To build my little love a home?

Up yonder, in the clean, sweet air
I think that I could keep her, there,
Too much an angel for the ground,
For Heaven somewhat too—warm and round.

DEEP WITHIN THE FOREST GRAY.

DEEP within the forest gray,
　　Sings a bird to the going day :
'Tis *her* song, lost as she passed that way,

Hark, the low wind in the firs !
In their tops it lightly stirs :
'Tis *her* sigh—ay, night, that sigh is hers.

Perfume gathers on the air,
Deep, rich heart of roses there—
'Tis *her* breath, sweet love herself, at prayer.

IN TWILIGHT LAND.

A MOUTH like hers you cannot doubt
  That Love himself designed;
The lips alway a little out
  From pushing sweet, behind.

The quiet moon rules yonder blue,
  Love lights her bluer eye:
Which heaven, which choose betwixt the two?
  For me—the nearer sky.

The face Hope sees leaned from above—
  That is her kind of face;
Movement to music born of love—
  That may suggest her grace.

Soft up and down the twilight land,

    From all the world apart,

—Although I hold her little hand—

    I lead her by the heart.

WAITING.

THE fields fold in silence the ripened sheaves,
The bright moon breaks on the swinging leaves,
The dark's great daisies are blowing above,
O, leap to my side, my Love—my Love !

You've said not a gem in the blue below
But, on my neck, it would lose the glow ;
You've said no bloom in the blue above
Is fit for my bosom, Love—my Love.

You've likened my song to the song of the bird,
My sigh to the tree's by the night wind stirred :
Like the moan of the pine, of the lone wild dove,
My song, my sighing, to-night, my Love.

The fields fold in glory the golden sheaves,

The full moon silvers the swinging leaves :

As the white cloud waits for the wind above,

I'm waiting for you, my Love—my Love.

THE OLD.

IT may be that the angels follow not
　　When we begin the varied round of days ;
While mothers lead along the early ways,
Not Heaven itself may add to childhood's lot.
Perchance God's envoys pass the viny spot,
The mossy couch, of youth—heed not the maze
Of dances where the dappling moonlight plays,
No burden to be borne, no battle fought.
The child, the youth, the man, angels go by.
May be ; but when life's biding shadows fold,
It must be that they hear, then, every sigh,
And gather lovingly around the old :
The glories on the going summer lie,
On the spent sun attend the hosts in gold.

OUR MOTHER.

WHEN the first man stood forth in Paradise,
    And the first woman came to grace her
        bowers,
The conscious garden glowed with thousand flowers,
With light—wild, laughing light, in thousand eyes
Of beauty.   Lovelier than young morning lies
On hill-tops, hovered round the wondering hours ;
And splendors richer than the red west showers,
Fell wide on Eden, all glory and surprise.
And does Our Mother love us, now, the less,
And why we fail her does she understand ?
For him that comes with trust and tenderness,
Eden still blossoms from her very sand :
Some flower—believe it—blossoming but to bless,
Will wait to wither in the last man's hand.

THE HEART'S SOVEREIGNTY.

I TEACH my feet, and they go not astray,
  My hands, and they reach not against my will ;
I can my eager ears with silence fill,
My tongue, so wayward—it, too, will obey,
And fickle vision, flown beyond the day,
Comes back to me, submissive ; ay, I chill
Fair pleasure to the quick, rude check the thrill
Of hope, and crying sorrow thrust away.
The lusty senses, full of youth, do yield,
Even wild-born thought does learn to heed my
    call ;
Fancy will leave her ever-vernal field,
Imagination share the toiler's thrall.
Ah, mocking heart, why do you let me wield
This master might, at last to baffle all !

DEATH'S.

WHEN hungry years youth's ruddy color drain,
    Glut them on his plumpness, suck dry his
      bones,
Choke laughter, song, with silence or with groans,
Put out his sight, over the jaded brain
Install disorder, break the old sweet strain
On his clogged tongue,—what is it? Death de-
    thrones,
But never honored age his sceptre owns :
Old men die not, they rest to rise again.
When lusty years youth's ruddy color feed,
Charge his clear eye with light, his veins with wine,
Honey his tongue, touch thought and feet with speed,
Build him, fill him, with shape and strength divine,
And he does drop and wallow, mire in greed—
Him Death marks: "Yonder—that one—he is mine."

THE GUEST.

A TRAVELER who had far countries seen,
   One summer day went roaming. By his way,
  At noon, school children leapt from books to play,
While the mistress looked adown the ringing green
After them : drawing near, the rider lent
His ready tongue to timely compliment.

At first the listener's thoughts fled in dismay,
   But soon the old peace fell upon her deep
   As on the flower before the Cave of Sleep ;
And of her neighbors and her flock at play
—Familiar themes, indeed, but never old—
In simple speech and fit the mistress told.

Lastly of her old father : it was he
   —She felt the blushes start—that stretched his hand
   'Cross broadest acres of the valley land.
The mistress answered all ; naught questioned she
More than the blossom asks whom it may greet
When the full air night-long unloads its sweet.—

Whether the work of will or destiny
   It boots not, nightfall found a stranger at
   The farmer's table.   Orator he sat
To beauty and gray hairs ; attentively
The old man listened, or in lusty tone
Matched some fine phrase with homespun of his own.

The morrow came, the guest arose to go.
   Then spoke the hearty host,—" A week lay by ;
   Young man, 'tis but the winking of an eye.
Home bodies, little of the world we know ;
Stay, tell us of the wide world widely seen :
Just up and down these ways our feet have been.

"You seek green pastures ; buy of me, and own
　　The richest in the valley.　Price—pay part
　　In money, part in cheer an honest heart
And seasoned wits withal, give mortals lone,
Tired of themselves.　Acres, I say, for cheer ;
Lay by—there 's a good twelve month in every year."

Biding his promised week, the guest delayed,
　　And bought him lands, and told of other climes.
　　His tales of countries far would many times
Return in waking visions of the maid,
Bringing a tremor such as breezes bring
Upon a moth sunning its pictured wing.

"Not yet, but in the happy after years ;
　　She will be older, then," the wanderer said.
　　Like the hurt flower that shuts its leaves in dread
Of passing clouds, she shrank before her fears,
In answer to his thought.　The hours went on,
The days, a rounded seven—the guest was gone.

One little week, but childhood's peace had fled ;
  The many summer murmurs, wont to be
  A ceaseless hymn of even harmony,
Now rose, unheeded.   "Nay," the maiden said,
" I hear the pines only of all the trees,
Their moaning, and that blown across the seas."—

The long, long summer went, and autumn came.
  Thick in the field stood, ranked, the stately
    sheaves,
  And apples peered 'twixt glossy orchard leaves ;
Nightly the low sun hung the vale with flame,
While winds were silent, and the darkened rill
Slipt noiseless as the mist along the hill.

The mistress, eve to eve, gazed on the sky,
  On its purple islands set in pearly seas,
  Its rich ships, steered between the mountain trees,
And, last, on the molten gold when suddenly
Came blushing up a rush of color, massed—
Swift, gorgeous ruin, and the daylight passed.

The sunset spelled her, now, as never before :
  'Twas at this hour the stranger held her hand,
  And loosed it, and went from her to the land
So far and strange. Oh, should she see him more ?
Would all be as it was ? What would he say,
Unsaid when like a king he strode away ?

With hope and doubt contending in her heart,
  Striving so deep within they made no sound
  Might pass her lips, she plied her daily round
Of cares, unswerving. All her daughter's part
She did ; and every little tongue would tell,
Unasked, she served the hamlet children well.

The days grew short, and round the cottage all
  Was white but the dull gray barns and black-topt
    wood :
  Still she was silent. Humoring his mood,
The father, half in jest, one night let fall
Inviting words : she tried to tell him—tried,
But only drew her closer to his side.

The wind was up, th' assaulted forest bowed,
  And rose again, defiant ; at the eaves
  Was fitful wailing—like a voice that grieves
For life-long hurt, the sound was ; high and loud
The passing blasts—a winter revel wild,
But cheerly by his hearth the old man smiled.

" Daughter," said he, "the spring is not so far
  Away but these blear eyes can see her green :
  Across the barren patch of weeks between,
She sets her feet this way.   God will, we are
To have the wandering scholar with us, then,
To brighten up us rusty farmer men.

"Suppose we keep him.   Girls will hang the head
  At old folks' notions.   Well, well, let it go ;
  You are too young yet, girl, I know—I know."
The other sought her chamber ; from her bed
She watched till the wind went down, and past the
    pine
The foxes trotted in the white moonshine.—

At last the dreary winter grays will go,

    Bring what it may, the April green will come ;

    Flowers for the altar, for the under home—

They bloom for either, and we cannot know.

The mistress—strange splendor hid her : so morn-

       ing light

Breaks round the star, and shines it out of sight.

The great sails filled along the windy main,

    The homing ships rode toward the western shore,

    But none there was the " wandering scholar " bore.

The spring, but not the stranger, came again ;

Ay, the May clouds came, and with the children

       wept,

Fostering the blossoms where the mistress slept.

THE CONFESSION.

FATHER, thy face were not so pale
   Did all thy flock together cry
Their sin.   Is 't, then, so hard a tale ?
  God's servant, what if, when I die
  —And that, perchance, before the eye
Of morn, fixèd on yon blue dome,
   Again looks light across the sky—
I should behold Hell's red mouth foam
With flutter of white souls thou hast chanted home ?

Hear me.   The path in anguish trod,
   That night, I once had loved it so !
Now, every root, and stone, and sod—
   How it did sting me !   To and fro

The strained trees gestured wild, as tho'
To mock me.   Repeating Arno's name,
   Upon this knife—long years ago
He gave it me—my cold hand came,
And drew and aimed it.   Instantly a flame

Of fearful brightness split the dark,
   The heavy-treading thunder fast
Marched up—the bright blade missed the mark.
   Methinks it knew Arno had passed
   That way, was by th' avenging blast
Driven to the wood, the brand of Cain
   Upon his forehead.   Loud and fast
The thunder strode, while my crazed brain
Made the thick drops my tears dashed back again.

—Dost catch it ?   Now a half-score years
   I 've heard that moan.—Hear me : hear it all.
If Arno spilled my life in tears,
   If I by Arno's hand did fall,

Why my sin weigh me till I crawl,
And he stoop not ?   What was 't but wrong
  For wrong ?   And had he sipped the gall
I fed on, lost to the gay throng
Where only joy's unmurdered hearts belong,

I had not done it.   I in my grave,
  What did he ?   Has the dove a wing ;
And Love—will he be cagèd save
  For first-love's hour ?—Heaven ! *there* to fling
  The flowers gathered of my Spring !—
The night the storm his daggers drew,
  And I drew with him, *she* did cling
To Arno's neck.   Oh, her breath blew
In my ears louder than the blast !—I slew—

—Hark—hark !   Teach it to say amen—
  That long last moan the dying make :
Between the thunder—again—again !—
  Nay, my good hand, you will not shake,

And, my good limbs, you will not quake,
So firm thro' all the storm's uproar.—
    Father, it is not fear does take
Such hold on me.—'Tis gone ; once more
I am the woman soldiers can adore.—

I go a doubtful way, so lack
    Thy blessing.   Strive not ; so 't shall be.—
The night closed in.   On darkening track
    The storm rushed up, clutched savagely
    The cow'ring wood, wrenched the strong tree
Till it did writhe for very pain,
    Moan, like a hurt beast, piteously ;
While the fierce thoughts in my poor brain,
Made the raindrops my tears dashed back again.—

But I have told thee, holding well
    To truth ; I have not learned to lie.
Useful, belike, the tale to tell
    Thy people, father, by and by.

Make clean work : tell them plainly why
I did it, no less plainly how.
   Say that I spoke unfalteringly,
That I kneeled not, nor once did bow
The head, nor on the lips take any vow.

I know 'tis rash.   As well I know—
   Mark me—when heaving earth shall thrust
Her dead up, and tossed coffins glow
   In long, forgotten sun, thro' rust
   Of ages will their throbbing dust
Break, burst, into the quick'ning air.
   On that great morning, Arno must
Stand forth—Arno, divinely fair—
Expectant 'mong the millions summoned there.

Swiftly past *her*, past all, will leap
   My lover, in his arms so strong
Once more to take me.   Embraced, we 'll weep,
   And all undo the olden wrong.—

Father, go back into the throng,
Tell them how brave was our good-by
Go back, and tell the coward throng
Thou saw'st the good blade do it.   Ay—
'Tis to the hilt—so—so.   Thy hand ; I—die.

WHO'S FOR THE MAGDALEN?

WHO'S for the Magdalen,
  Women and men?
Hold hands up.   One—two.
Fine lady, no, not you
Who said hard things;
Praise not her wings,
Now she's flown:
Remember you let her die alone.

" Who's for the Magdalen,
  Women and men?"
You heard it twice, thrice,
Some weeks since; but too nice
Those hands then.   Breath
Gone, now blind Death

Sees you kind :
She's dead, Ma'am—pray keep the fact in mind.

Who's for the Magdalen,
Women and men ?
What answer ?—"Ay !" "Ay !"—
Staunch churchman, tell no lie ;
Sepulchre white,
Wail not her plight
Now she's gone :
You gave her no bed to die upon.

" Who's for the Magdalen,
Women and men ?"
You heard it days, weeks,
It is since.   Kindness speaks
To live folk ; clay
Slights what you say,
Mocks your care :
That's only her body boxed, out there.

Who's for the Magdalen,

Women and men?

All hands up high, now

The death-damp's on her brow.

Till she went hence

A pestilence,

So unclean,

Why, now, is she better than she's been?

All for the Magdalen,

Women and men,

So sudden—"Ay!" "Ay!"—

There she goes, riding by,

Riding along,

She and her wrong,

Quite at ease;

The coaches are empty—look out, please.

Who's for the Magdalen,

Women and men?

As Heaven is true

Not one small soul of you !

It takes His heart,

Takes His God part,

That of yore

Said to her, *Go thou, and sin no more.*

THE EMPTY ARBOR.

OF a silent night in summer,
    Through her viny arbor bars
Looked a maiden as, above her,
    One by one, came out the stars.

While she gazed, a stealthy shadow
    Halted at the arbor door ;
And the music of the river
    Faltered, sank, and rose no more.

Raptured, she nor saw nor felt him,
    That dread shadow, black and still ;
Nor were missed the gentle measures
    Of the river 'neath the hill.

All unnoticed were the lilies,
  Leaned together on their bed,
And the roses' troubled slumber,
  And the words the night winds said.

Past the arbor ran the river,
  Round, the moon rolled up the sky ;
Slowly creeping toward the maiden,
  Closer did the shadow lie.—

As of old, the singing river
  Past the garden goes to sea ;
But forever and forever
  Shall the arbor empty be.

Still the summer vines are winding
  In and out the arbor bars
But the lifted face is missing
  At the coming of the stars.

Day to day the suns go over,

    Rose and lily come and go ;

But the shadow won the maiden

    For his bridal bed below.

THE WIND.

'TIS told, long years ago
    " The Wind—" a maiden cried,
" Bespeak him merry wedding ":
    That night the maiden died.

The Wind had won her spirit,
    Bride of the Wind was she :
And every breath blew sweet,
    The air grew melody.

O wondrous, wondrous night
    For Wind and Spirit fair :
The moon, the stars, the music,
    The bliss of the bridal pair !—

A life may all be lived
   'Twixt a sunset and a dawn ;
But pray for him that wakens
   To find the dream is gone.

A band of angels came,
   And bore the Soul away ;
On wings that none may follow
   They fled at break of day.

The lonely, homeless wind,
   He roves, bemoaning sore :
He seeks the Soul, a-roaming,
   A-moaning evermore.

SONG AND SILENCE.

IT is not on the evening air—
  The voice that day-long led the wind,
Trilling gay measures to the shades,
  Laughing frolic brooks behind.

The greenest mead, the bluest sky,
  Was brighter, warmer for its song ;
Time felt a quickening at his heart,
  Lighter danced the hours along.

Fresh blossom-voice, song-flower of light,
  God pity him it did not bless ;
But Silence, Silence—hear her, there,
  Her eternal tenderness !

THE TREES.

WHAT other shapes so stand, so fall?
   In every leaf uplifted,
Here greatness speaks, calm voices call,
   With gray years' vision gifted.

Men hope, and labor, and despair,
   Laughter they have and sorrow ;
The trees their gods' composure wear
   To-morrow and to-morrow.

SPRING SONGS.

I.

MY thoughts—they swing and chime
    I sing the swallows' joys
As sung, in olden time,
    The Rhodian chorus boys.

And here the wild birds sing,
    And there the wild flow'rs blow:
My heart—'tis on the wing,
    I know not where 'twill go.

II.

Now, back again to brown, gray hair,
    And honeyed be my tongue:

"Years do but cheat," says this sweet air,
   Who breathes it—he is young.

Hey, back again to brown, gray hair,
   Not all the songs are sung:
A sweetheart for the sweet Spring air,
   And my heart sweet and young !

III.

The maple and the birch were gray,
   I heard no happy song;
The grass was yellow, yesterday,
   Silence and dark were strong;

But, now, the black sky hurries blue,
   And brightness strikes the brown,
And dandelion 's reaching thro'
   To take his golden crown.

Ay, yesterday, I smelt the snow,
  To-day, the brooks make merry ;
The white is in the lowly blow,
  'Tis hiding in the cherry.

The alders and the hazels know,
  The violet understands :
On every side, above, below,
  Love calls, and claps his hands.

MORNING SONG IN SUMMER.

WHERE fairy fishers cast their net,
 And flee before the dawn,
Wave, webby mead with diamonds set,
 Shine wide—the night is gone.

Both happy ways and haunts forlorn,
 Hark, hear the woodland thrill !
The black flower blossoms—morn, new morn,
 Blows on the eastern hill.

Croon at the breast, sweet child-brook, croon,
 You 're Summer's, and we love you ;
Sing, sing, for dreams will fall at noon,
 From drowsy boughs above you.

Sing, too, heart ; for when shadows come,
   And touch and shut the daisies,
With very sweetness song falls dumb,
   Singing the Summer's praises.

SUMMER HOURS.

O WHAT bliss it is to be
　　'Neath a green old forest tree;
There to lie with open eye
While the dreams go gliding by !
Flit of wings and breath of flowers,
Follow, follow, Summer Hours.

Under shade of playing leaves,
With the visions fancy weaves—
Wary thoughts you cannot capture,
O, the wondrous, subtile rapture !

When the fitful breezes blow,
'Tis the thrill that lovers know ;

Either place it well may be,
In your heart or in the tree.

One by one, the dreams come on,
Now they 're glowing, now they 're gone ;
Meet them, greet them, while you may,
They 'll not come another day.
Flit of wings and breath of flowers,
Follow, follow, Summer Hours.

THE BROOK.

GAILY from yon shady nook,
  Hurry, laughing little brook ;
Thro' the meadows, round the hill,
'Twixt the willows by the mill,
Light and bright, and sweet and free,
Dance it, glance it, happily.

Not a trouble, not a care,
Finds you running—running, there.
Take, O take, your singing way,
Fair to-morrow as to-day ;
Light and bright, and sweet and free,
Wimple, dimple cheerily !

Gaily from yon shady nook,

Hurry, laughing little brook ;

Unlike you, 'neath golden sun,

Streams that in heart courses run :

Run, O, run afar from me,

Purl it, twirl it, merrily !

SUMMER NOON.

THE dust, unlifted, lies as first it lay
    When on his dewy path came up the day;

The spider-web stirs not ; on seas of air,
The thistle-ship, becalmed, rocks idly there.

The fern leaves curl, the wild-rose sweetness spends
Rich as at eve the honeysuckle lends ;

The creeping cattle feed far up the hill,
The blithest birds have hid, the wood is still ;

On daisied dials, pointing flower to flower,
The shadow-hands have reached the Golden Hour.

AUGUST DAYS.

SOFT and voiceless August days !
 Mute the ferny woodland ways,
Hushed the merry meadow lays ;
Stillness all and heavy haze
Of the charmèd August days.
In the hollow, on the steep,
Dwells a silence long and deep ;
Hush of slumber, lustrous haze,
Mellow, yellow August days !
Not the smallest whisper, now,
Of the secrets of the bough ;
In his glory hid, alone,
Sits the hill-god on his throne.
Voiceless August, soft and still !
Come, sweet dreams, and have your will :

No more sighing, no more tears,
They are ours—the Happy Years ;
Time 's gone backward, and life strays
In the olden golden days.

THE STRANGER-DAYS.

BUT yesterday the spirit came
    That sets the summer trees aflame :
I saw her fires when first they fell
On yonder flashing sentinel.
The gorgeous colorings that cloak
The sumach and the scarlet oak,
That in the ruddy woodbine glow,
That only lordly maples know,—
Here, one by one, I stood to see
Them glance and catch from tree to tree.
And now, that pomp not kings put on,
As in a night has faded—gone ;
And, motionless, a warning haze
Veils heavily the stranger-days.

GOING OF AUTUMN.

THE hearty portulaccas fade,
　　The scarlet salvias yield,
And soberest of hues are laid
　　On withered wood and field.

The first frosts at the wood's edge hold
　　Until the sun is high,
The golden-rod is waxing old,
　　Yes, dim the gentian's eye.

The kingfisher sits thoughtful, lone,
　　While, with a mournful smile,
The weak light leans on mound and stone
　　And dapple apple-pile.

No longer, now, the brooks rejoice,
The hours of joy are told :
Whither we list, a piteous voice
Says sadly, " I am old."

DEATH OF AUTUMN.

THEY have led her away,
   Up the stairs of day ;
Step by step in the mellow light,
Have led her away
To the turret gray
Where morning meets the night.
The ruthless band
Loosing her hand,
She throws her gorgeous garment down,
And with naked foot on her fated crown,
Leans and looks from the windows of air.
Long she looks below, above,
Then, to a sorrowful song of love,

Begins to bind her hair,
Strewn on her shoulders bare.

The keen winds cry,
As they cross the sky,
" Lo, our lady is nude,
And binds her hair in solitude ! "
The pitiless winds loud cry,
Round the turret whirling by ;
The withered leaves
And flowers—as she grieves
She flings them forth
To the bitter North :
Her heart's blood stains them all,
Bleeding—bleeding—as they fall.

'Tis night : the last pale leaf is kissed,
And cast down into the golden mist.
The keen winds cry,
As they cross the sky,

But Autumn has bound her hair ;

Ended her song of last despair,

And to and fro,

And to and fro,

Flit ghosts at the windows of air.

NOVEMBER.

THE summer blooms are lying
   Below the matted grass,
Through naked forest sighing,
   The winds of sorrow pass ;

The birds their flight have taken,
   No music by the way,
And each sweet haunt, forsaken,
   Yields fragrance of decay ;

Last splendors on the river
   Slow spread the parting sail,
Alone, the lank weeds shiver
   Before the with'ring gale.

FANCY'S FLOCK.

FANCY'S flock in dreamy close,
   Soft they rise when darkness goes ;
Tasting sweets of sun and shade,
Down the meadow, up the glade,
Here the field, and there the grove,
Now they rest, and now they rove.
Up and down all happy ways
Fancy's flock at pleasure strays,
Up and down, and far and wide,
Pretty shepherds at their side,
Some before, and some behind,
Lest they meet the chilly wind.—

Hark! the little silver bell!
Pretty shepherds, tend them well;
See there be no missing one
When the sunny day is done.

ON THE UPPER WAYS.

YOU 'VE climbed a steep, but have you gone
    Up Atlas with Endymion—
Been with him, there, as sung of old,
Moon-loved, herding his flocks a-cold?
You 've seen the sun come up and bound
The east with belt of red and gold ;
You 've seen, but have you trod, that ground,
The dancing-ground of th' early dawn?
Have you won those heights next the sun,
Where the wild-haired Bacchantes run?
You know the wood, but have you seen
Camilla in her tiger skin,
With arrow and with javelin?

You know the green fields and the trees,

But know you their divinities ;

Do you draw close as mortal can,

Dance with the nymphs that dance with Pan ?

You know by note the wild bird's song,

Where shadows lay them deep and long,

But what of that one song that dies

Upon the grave where Orpheus lies ?

You know the dews that gem the grass

Where white feet of the morning pass,

But the amber that is wept upon

The body of young Phaeton ?

The lily and the violet—

You 've seen, and plucked, and loved them, yet

There may be left the flowers to see

That on the plains of Enna be.

Ay, every field and every wood,

The gurgling stream, the murm'ring hill—

You love them as a lover should ;

But there be pleasures sweeter still

Along the viewless Upper Ways
The poet trod in olden days.
There, never is a fair shape found
But music floats it round and round ;
And fairest things that eye can see
Aye come and go in melody,
Until the last dull, halting thought
Is by the rapture swift upcaught,
And we do come a part to be
Of what we feel and hear and see.

THE POET.

FORTUNE does less capricious prove
   Than Nature : partial is Our Mother,
Making one poor to enrich another.
She gives a soul will no more move
Than it must with·rolling of the world,
Then a quick spirit that will be
Abreast with thought's infinity,
Urging, with colors wide unfurled,
The hard march starward.   From above
This one, sky-got, son of her love,
A wilding love-flower, blown
Into sweetness all his own.
Gentle, but with strength to stand
And meet the landscape's large demand,

The hills, towering upon his sight,

Lift him unto their noble height ;

The waters at his feet

Yield him their accent clear and sweet ;

His eye in darkness sightful is,

His ear can hear the silencies.

This is the poet, Nature's son

She sets her hope upon.

He knows where eyes are best,

There does most beauty rest ;

Therefore in forbidding places

Captures he most subtile graces.

The poet leaves no place the same

As when to it he came :

He something leaves, he something takes,

Now he destroys, now makes,

And all for truth and beauty,

To whom he owes perpetual duty,

To them and to no other.

Nature is a partial mother.

THE PILGRIMAGE.

RISE, soul ; we go to find
    That quiet land and kind
Where world and worry cease,
And spirits be at peace.
The years that make men old,
The buyer and his gold ;
Parading fools of fame,
In feathers of a name ;
The rubbish of vain strife,
The litter of mean life,—
All these will we forsake,
Our pilgrim's journey take.
Rise, soul ; we go to find
That quiet land and kind,

Far from the curse of care,

From darkness of despair.

There shall we wake or rest,

As eagles soar or nest ;

Shall ripen like the grain

Beneath free sun and rain.

Our labor to believe,

Our privilege to receive,

We shall not search, but see,

That which we would be, be

Rise, soul ; the hours fly on,

Make haste, let us be gone ;

The good land lies afar,

And we late pilgrims are.

THE SACRED VEIL.

THE fretting thoughts of toil had fled,
And a vision stood beside my bed.
A stately shape he was, and hoar,
In his right hand a staff he bore ;
Fine as mist-wreaths his beard and hair,
Drifting with lightest pulse of air ;
While a sober mantle, ample, free,
Heightened his native majesty.
He spoke ; and, to this hour, I hear
The gracious accents of the seer :

Mortal, the light crowning this hoary head,
Down gleaming ages, numberless, is shed,

It is the same that on creation's morn
Greeted your globe of night and chaos born :
I heard the star-song all that morning sung—
That wondrous morn when Time himself was
    young.
These hands, unlifted still thy race to bless,
Balanced the atoms struck from nothingness,
And gave them place ; when darkness opened
    eyes
I calmed the startled deep, hushed its surprise ;
When silence spoke, and unborn workmen heard,
I answered, first to serve th' Eternal Word.
We shaped the worlds, on paths of flaming gold
The distant suns into their orbits bowled ;
We fixed the limits of the reaching sea,
The wide air's boundary. As, to-day, they be,
In thy green earth these fingers set the seeds
Of life—seeds of the trees, of the wayside weeds:
Still does the first far purpose firm prevail,
Each follows his own kind, and cannot fail.

Mortal, to me fierce lightnings flash and die
Feeble and faint as glint of meadow-fly;
The storm-voice whispers, the wild cataract falls
Like evening shadows on your cottage walls.
I know the ways of silence and of sound,
Of light and darkness on their ceaseless round;
Th' interminable fields of space I see,
And, face to face, I sit with mystery.
To-night, O man ! thy quiet bed beside,
Stands one from realms to mortal quest denied,
The well proved servant of creation's God.
He brings this message :

                              On the meanest clod
Is Nature's every secret careful writ,
And peer of mine is he that readeth it.
But mad the mind that, in its searching, dare
Seek deeper than the treasure buried there ;
A fool's the fatal hope at last to part
The sacred veil before the human heart.

TOUNG TALOUNG.

STRANGER from banks of far Menam,
    First guest from Asia's sacred shrine,
Shall jesters answer gray Siam,
    The voice your land lifts up to mine?

'Tis Ava's court, not Laos' wood,
    Whose solemn accent overawes;
Proclaiming man's wide brotherhood,
    His varied lot, his common cause.

It says,—" Beneath this humble mien
    (Hast not believed as hard a thing?)
His lofty spirit may be seen
    That drank of wisdom at its spring.

" The patient one that went apart,
　　And, sorrowing, sought the Noble Way,
　Victorious Buddha, peace at heart,
　　Here bides ere passed beyond the day.

" Shall ye his mysteries deny
　　That never have his virtues known ?
　Well proved must be the wings that try
　　The upper air he made his own.

" Belief, long cherished, lends a power
　　The scoffer may not hope to touch :
　Ye are the people of an hour,
　　Know, therefore, ye must judge as such.

" Your step is light, your heart is young,
　　Not yet 'tis steepest where ye climb :
　Below us float the mists were hung
　　At morn of unrecorded time.

" Angkor—when was it she did build,
    Did all her thousand columns raise?
Whose fingers, as the Tuscan's skilled,
    There wrought, and shamed succeeding days?

" Cambodia's grasses—lo, they wave
    Over splendors Memphis never saw;
Nor moulds a hand in Theban grave
    Could teach her genius beauty's law.

" Before our shrines ye need not bow,
    To judge between us—that defer;
If ye are crowned with honor now,
    Look back—remember what we were.

" Look back, then forward cast your eyes:
    Perchance when ye are worn and hoar,
An infant race will shameless rise
    To mock the idols ye adore."

THE SILENT BLESSING.

GO thou and walk among the dead ;
   Sweet as deep
   Their endless sleep :
The hearts that erewhile, beating, bled,
Are stopt, by peace eternal tenanted.
  So quietly they keep
Their lowly bed,
Go thou and walk among the gentle dead.

The bitter word is as unsaid,
  Evil thought
  Can reach them not ;
If once in paths of error led,
Now are the mother arms of pity spread.
  It is a blissful spot :

With reverent head
Go thou and stand beside the quiet dead.

The very light seems softer shed
   On the tomb.
   Its flowers bloom
As though the sleeper's soul, not fled,
But lingering near, their conscious colors fed:
   They breathe as they perfume,
Soul-hallowèd,
A precious message from the friendly dead.

O, last of all, rest-tenanted,
   From this home
   Will spectre come !
Ghosts glide from out the live man's bed,
Not from their sleep untouched by joy or dread:
   No, never more they roam
That lay the head
To rest on peaceful pillows of the dead.

Go, take the blessing of the dead ;

  Draw thee near,

  And, listening, hear

The brave words by the silence said

To still the soul elsewhere unanswerèd :

Ay, heed that accent clear—

With bended head

Receive the benediction of the dead.

IN THE LANE.

A ND art thou then, my heart, too old
　　Ever to leap with love again,
To feel the strong blood-torrent rolled
　　Through heaving breast and teeming brain?
Is it no more, my heart, for thee
Life's one unquestioned ecstasy?

Are faded quite those dim, far days
　　When music mothered every sound,
When up and down youth's happy ways
　　Fared glories on eternal round?
Has chill of years killed every joy
That blossomed for the wandering boy?

'These are the trees once known so well
    We felt to them all but beknown ;
Their very shadow we could tell
    From others by the forest thrown.
The same glad songs from bush and bough—
As once we heard, we hear them now.

And these sweet flowers beneath my feet,
    Their young eyes greet us as of yore.
The hope, there ! Still they think to meet
    Her glance that shall not answer more :
To us alone it cannot be
They 're looking up so tenderly.

This is the same gray path we took
    Behind the slowly going day;
As they do now, the light leaves shook
    When evening breezes blew this way;
And there 's the glow upon the dome,
And here the cows are coming home.

Ah, no, good heart, thou still canst stir,
  Still lives the love first bid thee leap :
Still are we at the side of her
  They laid away 'neath yonder steep.
Though clods be on her and a stone,
In the dear old lane we 're not alone.

SONGS.

I.

GOOD BY.

IT is late, they must not wait,
 Standing by the wicker gate;
So she gives her little hand,
Gives her little dimpled hand:
" A kiss," he says, " pray, not a sigh,
 And sweet, my girl, good by—good by ! "

Night to night, and day to day,
Run the summer hours away;
Moon to moon, and sun to sun,
Merry, merry do they run;

Still, still she answers with a sigh,
His, " Sweet, my girl, good by—good by ! "

Light he said it, and was gone,
But she hears it echo on ;
She must hear it ever so,
Hear it though he never know ;
Ay, her last breath will, answ'ring, sigh,—
" Good by, my Love—a long good by ! "

II.

BY AND BY.

WHERE blossoms grow,
       And winds are low,
And brooks run lightly by,
There would we be,
'Neath a greenwood tree,
My Love and I—
My Love and I.

But Fate says, " No ";
He hates us so
That it were vain to try.
We 'll never be
'Neath the greenwood tree,
My Love and I—
My Love and I.

But, O, one day
We 'll steal away ;
We 'll cheat him, by and by,
Asleep all sound
'Neath a mossy mound,
My Love and I—
My Love and I !

WHAT'S IN THIS CHRISTMAS DAY?

WHAT'S in this Christmas day?
    Let Time's hoary warders say.
The Saxon grim—
There 's some of him ;
The Druid's hand is here,
The Greek and Roman cheer :
From East and West
Is gathered of the best,
From the new and from the old—
All the glorious day will hold.
From whitest sands to lichened rock
The doors of Hope unlock,
The gates of Peace swing wide,
At coming of bright Christmas-tide.

Saturn's temples fair
Are glistening in the air,
Thor's huge torches flare
In the dark forest, there ;
And, hark ! from sea to sea
The rouse of Bacchus breaks
Upon the quiet till it quakes
With revelry.
From the olive to the oak,
With blithe and mighty stroke
Bells of the ages ring,
And the little children sing :
For the lifting of the yoke,
For the giving to the poor ;
For that all-excelling art,
The building of the heart ;
For the good that shall endure—
For the sure and lasting good
Of a common brotherhood—
The bells of centuries ring

In a song

Loud and long,

And the little children sing.

The bands of holly bound,

The wreaths of ivy wound

On brow and pillar; pine

And fir—all from the mother ground

That speaks of hope—how they twine

It as they sing,

How proudly wear it as they bring

From heaven's height,

Tidings of delight !

Wind the holly crown,

Bind the ivy down ;

From soul to soul

Send round the brimming bowl ;

Drink deep, and sing

As the proud bells swing,

As the loud bells ring :

"Chime—chime—chime,
'Tis Christmas-time ;
Over the earth
Mercy, hope, and mirth !"

The pagan—shut him not away ;
This is the wide world's day.
All have their part—the dead, the live,
They that have striven, they that strive,
On rising wings,
Toward better things.
Day-long let joy go on ;
And when the splendid sun is gone,
Set the candle and the brand
Aflame from land to land !
Hope all round us wide and high,
Clear and perfect as the sky—
Hope, strong hope that cannot die,
Welcome the pagan to his part
In the building of the heart :

Nor time nor space shall dare divide,

Nor race nor faith, nor aught beside,

Children of men at Christmas-tide !

Let help who can

That bears the name of man,

Help in his chosen way

To keep this festal day.

But over other glories all,

Shining high and far,

Lo, the stopt, regardful star

Above the cradle in the stall !

Where the angels met together

With shepherds in the shining weather—

There 's the fountain of this song,

Song of ages, sweet and strong ;

Thence the deathless voice

That bids the world rejoice,

Thence the loosing of the slave,

The conquering of the grave.

Who shall heed what Sorrow saith ?

Who tremble at the name of Death ?

Swing—swing—

Hear the great bells ring,

And the little children sing !

The gates of Heaven are standing wide—

'Tis glorious Christmas-tide !

GREAT IS TO-DAY.

OUT on a world that 's gone to weed !
    The great tall corn is still strong in his seed ;
Plant her breast with laughter, put song in your toil,
The heart is still young in the mother soil :
There 's sunshine and bird-song, and red and white
    clover,
And love lives yet, world under and over.

The light 's white as ever, sow and believe ;
Clearer dew did not glisten round Adam and Eve,
Never bluer heavens nor greener sod
Since the round world rolled from the hand of God :
There 's a sun to go down, to come up again,
 There are new moons to fill when the old moons wane.

Is wisdom dead since Plato 's no more,
Who 'll that babe be, in yon cottage door?
While your Shakspeare, your Milton, takes his place
     in the tomb
His brother is stirring in the good mother-womb :
There 's glancing of daisies and running of brooks,
Ay, life enough left to write in the books.

The world 's not all wisdom, nor poems, nor flowers,
But each day has the same good twenty-four hours,
The same light, the same night.   For your Jacobs,
     no tears ;
They see the Rachels at the end of the years :
There 's waving of wheat, and the tall strong corn,
And his heart blood is water that sitteth forlorn.

EVERY ONE TO HIS OWN WAY.

OAK leaves are big as the mouse's ear,
    So, farmer, go plant.   But the frost—
Beware, the witch o' the year
    Her breast hath crost !
The bee is abroad, and the ant,
Spider is busy : ho, farmer, go plant.

The wind blows soft from the sailless sea,
    So, merchant, rig ship.   But the wave—
Beware, salt water can be
    A cruiser's grave !
Bring silks for milady, make trip
For wines and spices : ho, merchant, rig ship.

I heard round oath at the churchyard door,
  So, preacher, go preach.   But the Book—
Let not staff handle twist more
  Than shepherd's crook.
A Heaven and a Hell within reach,
And time spares no man : good preacher, go
  preach.

Go till the fields, and go ride the sea,
  Go solace or torture mewed folk ;
From frost and storm be you free,
  And Devil's joke.
I 'll sit in my doorway, God please,
Quietly looking between the green trees.

THE GOOD OLD-TIME.

WHAT worth have your mansions, your gold
    and your glory,
  When the thought, the heart, is away,
Somewhere betwixt the lintel and shingles
  Of a cot of a by-gone day ?

A gray old orchard, scarred as by battle,
  Stiff poplars out there, before,
Dandelions, lilacs, and no-name roses,
  And the pewee over the door ;

Staunch weeds, and grasses that challenge the winter,
  Wild cherries, red ripe on the wall,
The song of the birds in the hush of the morning,
  At evening, the low cattle-call ;

Savage paths a-bristle with burdock and thistle,
 Strong sun, and shadow as strong,
Quick brooks that learn the song of the upland,
 And sing it the still night long ;

Dewdrops and daisies, green grass and the robins,
 All glitter and twitter and sweet
From the cloud and the mist that meet on the moun-
  tain
 To the spider-nets under the feet ;

The clover, the laughter, the chat in the shadow,
 The noon horn's lusty alarm,
The halting mower, with a stroke at the sweat bee,
 Slow dropping his brown bare arm ;—

What are your mansions when these come and fash-
  ion
 Their dream wonders, day by day,
Weaving spring and summer and autumn together,
 In their own dear wayward way ?

The march is forward, the past is in ashes,
   From the old like a flame springs the new ;
But the boy in my heart with a shout will follow
   Where the mowers swing out in the dew.

GRANTHER.

A GRAND old man,
 Built after the olden plan ;
A muscular body, a massive head,
A man to be with till his years are fled,
A man to remember when dead :
 His smile, the wise look
 From the chimney nook,
 Where he whiffs and he whews
 While I read him the news !

 "Who 's killed, to-day ?"
 He asks in his ancient way ;
"And what have they stolen, this time, my lad ?
The rascals, they push it like pusley, egad :
Bad works, boy, bad—very bad !"

The pipe gets a slide
To the other side ;
How he puffs it and whews,
Keeping up with the news !

A character !
When he opens, " I tell ye, sir,
There 's nothing like knowing cheese from chalk,"
Or, "Square-toed, young man, if you're goin' to
    walk,"—
It 's none of your modern talk.
Run the text as it may,
He 's something to say,
Be you never so clever,
Will squelch you forever

He 's so complete
From the crown of his head to his feet,
Close grained, through and through of good oak
    stuff.
" Nonsense," he says ; "no trouble so tough
But good back-bone is doctor enough."

He 's the heart of the farm,
Still its strong right arm :
How he smiles and he smokes
Between sermons and jokes !

A SAINT OF YORE.

THERE lived of yore a saintly dame,
    Retired of life, unknown to fame,
Whose wont it was with sweet accord
To do the bidding of her Lord.
In quaintly-fashioned bonnet
With simplest ribbons on it,
The neighboring folk remember well
How prompt she was at Sabbath bell.

I see her, now, her decent shawl,
Her sober gown, silk mitts, and all ;
Again I see her with a smile
Pass meekly up the narrow aisle.
The deacons courtly meet her,
The pastor turns to greet her,

And maid and matron quit their place
To find her fan or smooth her lace.

Of all the souls that worshipped there,
She best became the House of Prayer :
Her gracious presence—from it beamed
The light that robes the Lord's redeemed.
That gentle mien did often
Some "hardened sinner" soften,
Whose thought had else turned light away
From rigid lesson of the day.

Her eyes, with reverent reading dim,
Sought neither chapter-page nor hymn,
She knew them both ; and as in song
Her voice kept evenly along,
'Twas not so much like singing
As like the music clinging
About some sacred instrument,
Its lessening breath not wholly spent.

Still, one by one, the good folk fill
The little church upon the hill—
The little church with open door,
Just as it stood in days of yore,
The grass around it growing
For nearest neighbors' mowing,
The row of battered sheds behind
Ready to rattle with the wind.

Old Groveland Church !   I mark it well,
From weathered steps to belfry bell.
Few changes, there ; but in yon ground
Have thickened fast the slab and mound.
Hark !   Shall I join the praises ?
Rather, among the daisies,
Let me, in peaceful thought, once more
Be silent with the saint of yore.

THE OLD FARM BARN.

THE maples look down with bright eyes in their
    leaves,
The clear drops drip from the swallow-built eaves,
The chickens find shelter, the cisterns fill ;
There 's a busier whirr from the wheels of the mill,
The pond is all dimples from shore to shore,
And the miller smiles back from his place in the door ;
Slow mists from the mountains come drifting down,
The houses show fainter afar in the town,
The gust sweeps up, dies away again,
Then, loud and fast, the rap-tap of the rain :
For all yonder sun 'tis my heart's rainy day
In the old farm barn, with the children at play.

The oxen chew slowly, with sleepy eyes,

The huddling sheep shrink to half their size,

The dazed calves stare at the dingy wall,

Old Nancy looks soberly out from her stall,

Tiger Puss crouches close to the mouse's hole,

Cæsar gnaws boldly a bone that he stole—

Over all, the roof and the dance of the rain.

Not a sorrowing thought, not a touch of pain ;

The old farm barn is so dusk and still

The spiders sleep on the window sill :

'Tis the hush, the drowse of the rainy day,

And I 'm leaping again from the beam to the hay.

Up, chunky George of the woodchuck race !

Hist, withy Ben, with the chipmunk face !

This way, broad Bill, with the trousers wide !

Come, stumbling Tom, with the big toe tied !—

The scramble is made up the shaky stairs,

Hatless and breathless, we stand in pairs ;

Bawling Bob gives the word, and down we go

From the cobwebbed beam to the bay below.
The sport is forbidden, hence double the zest ;
More risks than the damage to breeches or vest :
Aha ! he 's no coward gets sprout, to-day,
For bliss of the leap from the beam to the hay !

Oh, the way of the world, its worry and strife—
The wrestle, the battle, that men call "life" !
On us all, at times, may the noon sun shine,
It may warm to your heart, may warm to mine,
But the joy long gone, though never so small,
Compared with joys present, is worth them all.
The future we know not, but safe is the past,
And the first we loved we love to the last ;
The dearer gifts, the longer we live,
Are the quiet joys our memories give :
Ay, back, my heart, to the rainy day—
To the old farm barn and the children at play.

AUTO DA FÉ.

HEIGH-HO, a drowsy, drippy day
    Suits well your single gentlemen
Whose locks begin to show the gray.
The grizzly drizzle round my "den"—
'Tis sent on purpose, I dare say,
For bachelor's *Auto da fé.*
I have the ribboned missives, here,
The hearth flames flicker low, but clear,
The spell is on—the savage spell
To do the burning quickly, well:
So, to it.
        Heavens! how old *am* I?
It seems a hundred years since she
That inked this paper said to me,
" You will be older, by and by."

I was a beardless rover, then,
With dreamy brain, and ready pen,
At sight of form or features fair,
To write a ditty of despair.
Well, Constance, I am older, now ;
And you?   The marble of that brow
Must have its channels deep and bold ;
High time that love 'twixt us was cold.—
Spring up, you little tongues of fire,
For I begin the precious pyre.—

These?   These from stately Margaret.
I never loved her, never ; yet
There was a something us between
That keeps a spear of memory green—
A plucky, strong, unbrothered blade,
Still smiling in its depth of shade.
Well trained the hand that down this page
Drew line to line ; each letter clear

And firm from " Honest John, my dear,"

Far as the awkward word, "engage."

"Engage," again !   Did I propose?

"Engage " !   I 'll read on to the close.—

Tall Margaret, if this be true,

In those young days what didn't I do ?

For shame !—Up, up, good flames ! To you

I toss this ample package, too.—

There 's nothing like a rainy day

When one would put old loves away :

Between the water and the fire,

The fated passions soon expire.

Ha, this snug bundle—what an air

Of pride about it !   What a care

To make a fellow bite the dust :

" Down on your knee, you must, you *must!* "

And probably I did go down,

—General prostration seized the town—

In fact, I know I did ; but, then,

Somehow I found my feet again.

A girl 's a girl, a boy 's a fool,

And life—it proves a sorry school.—

Imperial Fair (for thou *wert* fair

As any breathing lower air),

I do forgive all injury

Thou didst to either heart or knee.

I spy a word, now here, now there,

That shows you could a little " care ";

Right royal Lois, 'tis too late.—

Receive these proudly, gentle grate.—

And now, to Helen.   Taste of wine

Is on my lips, and all sweet spices :

This dark-eyed one had been divine

But for some few mundane devices.

She traced these pages sharp and fast

As hailstones drive on the winter blast :

Tame passion Helen never knew,

A very hurricane she blew,

Or sat in midst of awful calm.

No other ever sang a psalm

As she could sing it, on occasion ;

Another's eyes did never play

Such pranks after the operation.

'Twas hard to know which way to take her,

But rare the wooer would forsake her

For charmer of a surer mind.—

Angel with a dash of the tiger kind,

Love's leopard—Helen, off and on,

We loved it madly, years agone !

When you were married—

                    Blaze, bright pyre ;

I add these, also—fire to fire.—

And still the rain, the gray, gray rain ;

And there 's that last year's leak again.—

Rustum, why can't you bring a pail

'Twixt swings of that eternal tail ?—

'Tis almost done ; one offering more.

What says the clock ? Quarter of four.—
Rustum, old fellow, foul or fair,
You 're right : we 'd better take the air.—
These last—these little yellow scraps,
Good fire, ere long, perhaps—perhaps.

AN EPISTLE TO A BACHELOR.

"RESOLVED, at last, to woo and wed : "
　　This ill accords with what we said
In those triumphant days, old fellow,
When, with good " Park and Tilford " mellow,
Health after health went round the "den,"—
" Here's to all single gentlemen ! "

Though not so strange as it first appears,
(Grave Horace fell at fifty years)
Still, as I read on, sombre hues
Did follow, bordering on the "blues,"
And sounds, as when the late leaves stir,
Crept heartward from the days that were.

The hint is dropt with caution nice,
You 'd not despise a bard's advice :
Accept some facts as one may hand 'em,
Not without thought, but still at random.

Sweet Eve, ensconced 'neath Eden's tree,
Inducted woman's ministry ;
Potent not only over Adam,
But, fast as after mothers had 'em,
Reaching each son of every race
Destined to grievance or to grace.

This doctrine courses Sacred Writ,
And pagan lore continues it :
Beloved of gods, high Hebe stumbled—
Again was heavenly woman humbled.
Thence down, pursue her where you will,
The first grand failure follows still.

Let me be last to slight the pearl
That glistens in the dimpled girl ;

But, ah, it tarnishes with years,

At length in dullness disappears.

Ever from April to October

Does transient beauty hasten sober ;

And, finally, in dread November

Comes unconditional surrender.

The brightest shiner in the brook

Is an ugly wriggler on the hook ;

A star the fire-fly sparkles by,

Get fingers on it, 'tis—a fly.

At least have cunning of your cat :

He 's fond of fish, but, for all that,

No trout can tempt him in deep water

As you must wade for beauty's daughter.

——O beatific solitude

Where only bachelors intrude,

While round the edges of your shade

Inspiring moves th' occasional maid !—

William, so earnest, able, true,

I prophesied high deeds for you :

I deemed you would a banyan be—

A noble forest in one tree,

Huge protest 'gainst all huddling men.

I thought you 'd teach the world that when

The solitary seeker calls,

Some Newton's apple timely falls,

That lamp of Galileo swings

For them that think, alone with things.

The wisest of all brutes that be,

Breeds not in mean captivity :

Genius is not gregarious, Will.—

And here a pause to point my quill. . . . . . .

How villainous to so defame

Sweet innocents with touch of blame !

I 'll play the hypocrite no longer.

'Twas thus we put it—only stronger—

In days by-gone.   Changed, changed since then

The tyros of the Broadway "den."

"Onward, onward to something better !"
  Now cries the writer of this letter.
  The dears shall be no more derided :
  Say prayers, my boy, and—do as I did.

BROTHER BACHELOR BATRACHIAN.

"——wears yet a jewel in his head."

HO, hermit of the cellar wall,
    If you are coming out at all,
Come now ; in thirty minutes more
The rain will trickle down your door.
Make haste, my boy ; this ceaseless drizzle
Would prove most friendship sheerest fizzle,
But we old jovies, once together,
Have nought to fear from wind or weather.
Come, come ; hurrah, there, bachelor lump !
Betwixt a waddle and a jump,
Judge-like ascend your own toad-stool
Worked out last night by wizard's tool.

Ha, there you are, sedate as ever ;
Prodigious plain, but passing clever.
The years are twenty to a day
Since you and I first sat this way ;
How many more think you to squat,
Contented, on our pleasant spot ?
Be frank with me, you wily monk,
Impervious, solemn, clumsy chunk !

What mischief are you plotting, now,
Squaring about Sou'-West by Sou' ?
A weather-cock with half the pains
Can nose precise a dozen rains.
Be seated.   It is rather cold
Way down there in your stony hold?
Those dungeon vapors—don't you think
They make the spirits sort of sink,
Partic'larly when stingy fate
Too long withholds the cheery mate ?

Let go in peace that fiftieth fly ;

Another morsel, and you die !

With your last testament unsigned,

How dare you gorge yourself stone blind ?

A risky situation that

When toads are twenty-odd, and fat.

Feel nervous, fellow ?   Pshaw ! lean back,

And from your buff aldermanic sack

Puff out the truth for once and all :

Your mind's made up to wed, this fall,

Good year ; whatever comes to pass,

The insects in the garden sauce

Alone, I 'll guarantee to load

With plenty all the tribe of toad.

My hand, old dumps ! a worthy wife

Will lift you to a higher life :

The dumb inflation of that cheek

Will yield to maxims Solons speak,

In pleas for daily peace and ease

You may prove second Socrates.

Why, one lone toad down in the wall,
Is a wart heap, no toad at all.

There—don't repeat that deac'nish wink;
I·know exactly what you think.
Somebody (not far off) has had
His youthful frolics, good and bad,
His salad antics : dare he vow
He's got well over 'em ?   How's that—how?
Warm evenings, just outside the walk,
Those cooings by the cabbage stalk !
Droll chap, I grant you're old and fat,
And may have nieces and all that ;
But when with *her* you claim relation—
Blood ties remotest in creation,
I'd have you know it won't go down
Though backed by every toad in town.

Sit still, no offence: I can't help joking,
Moment I see that stub nose poking

Into the light.   *You* take a mate—
Prepost'rous !—   Certainly ; too late.
At your age, better a hangman's halter
Than the kind they 're led with to the altar.
Heaven spare the storms that we can't weather,
We two old jovies, here together.—

Heigh-ho, the gentle, misty rain
Is coming down the hill again.
Did you perceive just what was meant
'Bout that Last Will and Testament ?

Grave Bachelor Batrachian, pray
What sense in sidling off that way ?
Ridiculous old rogue !   Turn round,
You baggy wag from underground !
No other eyes see well as mine
How bright your inner riches shine :
Long may they live when you are dead—
Leave me the jewel in your head.

OUR OPHIDIAN FRIEND.

CYLINDRICAL thing
    Without leg, without wing,
Glazed membrane stuffed with motion,—
I hold the heretical notion
That because you crawl
Is no reason at all
For laying so odious stress
The length of your lowliness
    A walk or a glide,
    A stride or a slide,
    A trip or a slip,
    A skate or a skip,
    It's one and the same to me,
    Sly, India-rubber iniquity !

And as to your morals, there, too, I 've suspicion

We harp overhard on the point of position.

I admit you do things not precisely right—

It 's rather erroneous, for instance, to bite—

But we all have our lapses, perhaps full as serious

As those at your threshold, twister mischievous.

To travel way back to the start of the world,

When in grasses of Eden your ancestors curled,

Resurrecting malfeasance from time out of mind,

Limp ringler, I say it 's a little unkind.

Suppose in snakeskin a wretch did deceive

The lady initial, ingenuous Eve ;

In their own skins, to-day, that 's exact what men do,

Then put the whole blame (and the bludgeon) on you.

Your forefathers, likely, were up to their tricks,

But the fault, after all, was plainly Old Nick's ;

And if only *your* paths are sinlessly slid,

Why should we care a rap what your granddaddy did ?

Poor animate string of the glittering eye,

If you 'll look to your head, to my heels will I :

As for me and my house, we 'll never inveigh

'Gainst a ribbon that harmlessly garters our way,

Nor with cudgel from cactus or Calvin hewed,

Fall thwacking its limber longitude.

   Abused, abjured Ophidian,

   Bask on in peace meridian ;

The more of the tale of the Tempter they make,

The closer I 'll hold to the tail of the snake.

SILVER BELL.

A FAR, in scarred Nevada,
   There sat in the smoky gloom,
A group of riotous outlaws,
   'Round Rennigan's gambling-room.

They had won and lost and settled,
   Forgot the dice and cards ;
And now they drank, and storied
   Of foes and doughty " pards."

The storm was at the maddest,
   With oaths and laughter-blast,
When into their midst ('twas morning,
   Three o'clock and past,)

An old man crept from his corner ;
　Weighing each braggart word,
He sat there, bowed and silent,
　A-nodding as he heard.

Sat silent till fierce Bigglin,
　Glancing from guest to guest,
Cried, " Clash with me your glasses,
　The ' shot of all the West ! ' "

Then spoke the old man, shaking
　His long locks, loose and white,
" Hold, there !　Bold words and hasty ;
　Wait till the morning light."—

" Old chap, no more ; you 're rattled,
　There 's dry stuff in your brain ;
Open and wet your whistle,
　Nor let it blow again."

So jeered young yeasty Bigglin,
    Filling the old man's glass.—
" I 'll drink ; and you—you will listen
    To what once came to pass.

" Here 's health to you, young Bigglin,
    Live long—till you be wise ! "
The old man drank, and faced them,
    The fire tonguing up in his eyes.

" You 've heard of Battle Mountain,
    The home of Silver Bell ;
'Tis there they tell a story
    And that 's the tale I tell."

They stopt him, filled their glasses—
    " Both names—we know 'em well.
The lass of Battle Mountain,
    Drink, drink to Silver Bell ! "—

" Ay, drink ; but had you known her,
　　Felt her black hair, wave on wave,
　That caught with the crush of the serpent,
　　And held with the strength of the grave !"—

" Hear him !　So you, too, loved her,
　　Before your pulse was gone.
　And still on top and hearty :
　　Bravo ! old man, go on."—

" The guess was easy.　Loved her?
　　I loved her, loved her well :
　Love followed, close as her shadow,
　　Fawn-footed Silver Bell.

" But I must keep to my story
　　Of two, you understand,
　Two lovers who, belting their pistols,
　　Went up to seek her hand.

" ' What !   By blue heaven,' exclaimed she,
  ' Come you to shoot me down !
I 'll whip my pretty pearl-hilt,
  And march you back to town.'

" Low bowed Nevada's Marksman,—
  ' We come to see how well
We can cut a gray hawk-feather
  From the hand of Silver Bell.'

" At the side of his haughty rival,
  Low bowed young Shooting Star,—
' Safe the little brown fingers ;
  You know what shots we are.'

She took the gray hawk-feather,
  And tossed her round, bare head,—
' What if you nick a finger ? '
  ' We 've fixed that point,' they said.

" She twirled and twirled the feather
    In that small hand, like the cone
Of the fir in its turn and taper,
    And brown as the brown madrone.

" Firm, then, the trim deer-ankles ;
    With the feather at arm's end,
She stood and waved them backward
    To the shade of Hazel Bend."—

" I' God's name, which first tried it ?"
    The Kid of the Cliff shrill cried.—
" The lot fell to the Marksman—
    The girl's hand to her side."—

" Coward ! he struck a finger."—
    " Touched one ; but a coward—stay.
The second shot he bettered
    The aim at the feather gray :

" He turned the muzzle homeward,
　　And like a clod he fell "—
" By God "—" Hold ! the feather,
　　Once more, for Silver Bell.

'' Again 'tis floating—ready !
　　This time 'tis harder far :
　　See how the light thing trembles !
　　Steady, Shooting Star.——

' 'Twas cut nice in the middle ;
　　And ere the slim tip fell,
　　Lithe as a hound leapt forward
　　The winner of Silver Bell :

'' ' Brown beauty, blind was the bullet—
　　A clumsy shot,' he said ;
　　But my Marksman paid dear for it,
　　In the shade of the hazels—dead.'

" The stare of the girl was savage
    As a panther's on the prey,—
' There 's the hand : a wound, and no bleeding?'
    She had pressed the blood away.

" Slow back she stept, and halted,
    And at her heart aimed well :
Will you give over or claim it—
    The prize of Silver Bell?'

" ' Go free,' he said ; ' 'twas the other !
    I 'll take my way afar.'
And never saw she thereafter
    The face of Shooting Star.

" She never saw him thereafter,
    Nor has he shot from the day
He cut the gray hawk-feather,
    And took his lonely way."——

The old man stopt, still eyed them,
Smoothing his weapon bright,—
" As gray as the gray hawk-feather,
There comes the morning light.

" You all are young, all shooters
Let two come out the door
That think it safe to face him—
Old Shooting Star, once more."

So passed he into the morning,
Still turning from afar ;
But no man chose to follow,
A target for Shooting Star.

HELEN.

ON certing subjects I jest know :
    There 's gals an' gals, I say,
An' the purtiest—don't care where you go—
   Lived yender, crost the way.

Them ankles, round as a rollin'-pin ;
   That braid which hung way down ;
All bright as if the day 'd struck in—
   A sky gal on the groun' ;

A leetle color on her cheek,
   Where the blood looks out o' door,
Like them fust changes on the maples
   From frost, the night afore—

No use in paintin' a snowdrift white,
    I needn't go no fu'ther ;
God might, I s'pose—I s'pose he might—
    But he never made another.

We warn't no more nor a year apart,
    I 'd watched her from a chicken ;—
I 'm there, right there, when you 're talkin' heart
    An' this 'ere women-pickin'.—

We learnt together. At a book
    I hedn't no special sconce,
But in lickin's—'stead o' her, I took
    The ruler more than once.

I 'd danced long wi' her rether reg'lar,
    At most the scrapes in town ;
Fact, I hev heerd 'twas feared I 'd shake
    The darned old tavern down.

I 'd helped her folks at killin'-time,
    Or when hay was late in cuttin' ;
An' when their eatin' warn't quite prime,
    Swapt a bit of veal or mutton.

As I said, we started head an' head,
    But she kept gainin' groun' ;
At last, my dander up, I said,
    " I 'll in, be it swim or drown."

So, 'rangin' on 't some evenin's prev'ous,
    One mornin' I hitched the pair ;
An', riggin' out my most mischievous,
    Druv her, spinnin', to the Fair.

To this 'ere time, to put it nice,
    There was nothin' wuth declarin',
'Cept I 'd kissed her onct or twice,
    At a huskin' or a parin'.

The grays, I swings ! they made things whistle,
   A-gittin' to the Fair ;
An', like a gold finch on a thistle,
   She sot beside me square.

As I was sayin', the grays warn't lazy,
   We got there bright an' early ;
The dew still glistenin' on the daisy,
   The hills with mist all curly.

It ain't my style—doin' things by halves,
   I cut the entire figur' ;
We took all in, from the colts an' calves
   To the patent thig-a-magigger.

Ball butter, punkins two foot thro',
   Turnips, an' cheese, an' honey,
Pink-eyes, rag carpets, an' patch quilts, too—
   We seen 'em ; an' I slung some money.

I scattered the coppers ; an' my pile,
   I remarked, I 'd willin' risk it
That a gal I knowed could beat 'em a mile
   On gingerbread and biscuit.

We heerd the speech an' lots o' the band,
   See the trot an' plowin' matches ;
An' I never so much as techt her hand—
   Though there was some close scratches.

We made a day on 't : see all the stock,
   The fruit, the home manufactur's,
An' got away at eight o'clock,
   'Thout any compound fractur's.

The air was closter than I need,
   An' gin me a sort o' chokin' ;
So I druv at no partic'lar speed,
   An' tried to pluck up, jokin'.

The makeshift didn't take, somehow,
   An', rether wuss than better,
Sez I, " I 'll bring things hum, right now ;
   If she mittings me—let her.

" Helen," sez I, a-takin' her hand,
   " Anent the fire-fly's spark,
That 's jest my fix—you understand—
   A-burnin' in the dark."

She sot as straight, sir, straight an' still,
   As a rabbit in the wood—
On top the choke I took a chill ;
   She certing understood.

" The goldenrods are comin' on,
   The sumachs growin' brighter,
The singin' birds hev quit, an' gone,"
   —I squeezed a leetle tighter—

"It's lonesome like (ez you be fair
    I know you 'll be forgivin'),
An' I 've a castle in the air
    Too big for *one* to live in.

"Since fust we played house-keep together—"
    Here come a flash o' lightnin' !
My back-bone felt like a big wet feather,
    But I kept my hand a-tightenin'.

"Ever since that day—" an' there I broke.
    So did a clap o' thunder :
It seemed as if the hevings spoke,
    An' I could see it stunned her.

She dropt them long, thick, sweepin' lashes,
    And her face grew white all over,
Like where a sprinklin' of wood ashes
    Brings up the new white clover.

I—guess we 'll let the subjeck drop.

Do you hear that youngster yellin'?

When he begins I allers stop,

Give the floor to him an'—Helen.

POETRY MADE PRACTIC.

(WITH APOLOGIES TO MR. STEDMAN.)

THE leaves are gettin' sere,
    The green is growin' gray ;
It 's been a tryin' day
At turnin' o' the year.

My spritely little fire,
It frisks it brisk as though
It sort o' seemed to know
A heart could kind-a tire.

I 'll hasp that swingin' blind,
And pull the curting down ;
It 's most too fur to town
Ag'in a nippin' wind.

I reck'n I better read
A bit o' poetry ;
A tech of love, may be,
To keep from goin' to seed.

Hello, what 's this chap at ?
" The Doorstep," eh.   That 's right ;
Not quite a doorstep night,
This 'ere, but what o' that ?

Steady—he 's not there yet.
The snow all crispy—good !
'Twixt " tippet " an' the " hood "
There 's suthin' up, I 'll bet.

Her " hand outside her muff "—
She 's fixin' plaguy quick ;
Well, now, that *is*, that 's slick—
A-hold on 't !   Good enough.

He 's posted how things goes
With country folks, I see ;—
Dern slumpy poetry
Onless a feller does.

Well said—I do declare !
The "old folks," " ringlets," "moon "—
He 's stickin' to the tune,
And must be almost there.

A fiddle on his " sister " !
Ef he should up and blunder—
No, by the jumpin' thunder !
He has—he 's kissed her !—

Thar 's poetry.—Down you, houn' !—
It ain't so very late ;
I 'm goin' to strike my gait ;
Yes, sir, I 'm off to town.

An' Mr. Pote—Git, Rover !—

Ef it would be amusin',

1 'll prove by me and Susin

Jest " who can live youth over."

THE TRAPPER'S SWEETHEART.

WIDE awake, now, mind your eye,
 She will think on 't by and by ;
She will see—perhaps—she may
'Gin to-morrer, not to-day.
 " Be true to me,
 Furgit," says she,
Jest as it may hit her fancy :
That 's it zackly, that 's my Nancy.

Take a squirrel up a tree,
Jest so frisky, sir, is she :
Now on this side, now on that,
You must watch her like a cat.
 It 's " No," it 's " Yes,
 I rather guess "—
Jest as it may tech her fancy :
That 's it zackly, that 's my Nancy.

You 've seen creeturs sudding lame,
Git too near 'em, an'—they 're game !
Her right over : an inch too near,
Up and off is Nancy dear.
　　" Yes, Jake," says she,
　　" Laws sake !" says she,
Jest accordin' to her fancy :
That 's it zackly, that 's my Nancy.

Whew, a gal 's a cunnin' thing !
You must take 'em on the wing.——
I 'll be goin' ; fur, ye see,
Nancy, she 's expectin' me.
　　I 'll hit or miss her,
　　It 's quit or kiss her ;
I 'm fur facts, while she 's fur fancy :
That 's us *zackly*—me and Nancy.

THE JOCKEY'S SOLILOQUY.

I WONDER what's got in 'em all,
  A-kitin' arter one :
Whoa! Young and old, and short and tall—
To see 'em break and run !
I vow, it's quite amusin',
Their thirty-gait enthusin'——
Come up, old Daisy, gal,
Come up, old lazy gal !

Gee off, I say, there—out the track !—
Great turnpike, how they come !—
Haul in, and take an easy shack ;
Miss Susin ain't to home.

Sich drivin' is abusin',

Sich thunderin' enthusin'——

Come up, old Daisy, gal,

Come up, old lazy gal !

Yes, sir, from gawky four-year old

To splinty, heavey hoss,

They 've struck a gait that they can't hold :

On Susin's track *I*'m boss.

P'r'aps hardly her own choosin',

Don't lay the blame on Susin——

Come up, old Daisy, gal,

Come up, old lazy gal !

Now, she warn't made for no junk cart,

She 'd take the bit, you see ;

But I jest broke her colty heart

'Thout scratchin' the single-tree.

So, now, of course, no trouble
To take and hitch her double——
Come up, old Daisy, gal,
Come up, old lazy gal!

She ain't to home, boys—out o' town ;
Some silver plate, you know,
And ribbons—Neighbor, good morn'n': ride
    down
As fur as the new *de-po?*—
Jehu ! this turnip's loosin' ;
She whistles ! That means Susin—
No dancin', there : well, well,
 You jealous Daisy, gal!

MODERN PROGRESS.

A FEW TECHES ON'T, BY AN OLD FOGY.

WE 'RE livin', now, in most trimendious times,
    Too wondersome for plain straight-furrid
      rhymes,
But, I confess, my poor old fogy brain—
It would jest like to ketch a glimpse, again,
Of some things they have whisked clean out of ken,
Upsettin' Natur' and my feller men.
The good old world, I s'pose, is still a ball,
And keeps a-rollin'; 'pon my word, that's all
Remains o' 't nat'ral.   Once upon a time
'Twas suthin' of a trip from clime to clime ;
But any ninny, now, can stand right here
And holler business in a Hindoo's ear.

With ingines, snapagraphs and howlephones
A-muddlin' up the very poles and zones!
Good Lord, is this still Adam's fallen race
So cool annihilatin' time and space,
A-drivin' of the coursers o' the air
As sainted granther did his sorrel mare!
But I would let old mother Natur' go
If they would leave the folks I used to know.
Why, them nussed at the breast of my nativ' lan',
Half on 'em talks sost I can't understan';
While them fresh critters from a furrin shore,
They 'd scared the geese at our old homestead door.
Now take, for inst', them rattin' almond-eyed—
I thought that sich lived clean on t' other side :
Bless ye, there ain't no t' other side, to-day,
Jess like 's not Boston 's sot on Bottany Bay.
The times is thunderin' wonderful, I know—
This ere a mixin' up creation so ;
But, by my bones! I 'd like once more t' enjoy
Them blessin's I was riz to from a boy.

I 'd like the reg'lar old religeon back,

Which said we jest must walk the narrer track,

And there an end on 't : now, where we 're to go

(Maybe some folks are smarter) I don' know.

My bible might as well be on the shelf ;

They 've found the world jest up and made itself,

And Christians, even, have fixed the Good Book over

Until there 's leetle left on 't but the cover.

No, faith, I 'll keep the track my fathers trod,

For all their Sheols and their Nothin'-God.

Great times, it seems, is made of rush and doubt,

But where the great comes in, I hain't found out.

If Natur's done for and religeon, too,

Pray leave me suthin a-ruther 't won't slump thro' !

Leave, say, a man will find spare time to sit

Him down in his right mind, and chat a bit ;

A plain, old-fashioned, homespun, mortal man,

Who allers takes it easy when he can.

Leave me a woman tendin' her own child,

A-lookin' like they used to when they smiled,

Not makin' on it ; leave a good cart-load

Of children which *is* children till they 're growed ;

Give me some gals, once more, can mind a kitchen,

And tend to suthin else besides bewitchin';

Some women-folks whose art ain't quite so high

They 're clamberin' up, a-frescoin' the sky ;

Leave boys not all base-ball, or else afloat

In tooth-pick of a college racin'-boat—

Some square-backed boys with heads on, not them
    cranes

From York, with a teaspoonful of bran for
    brains ;

Leave me a story-book, 'fore I begin it !

I know for sure that there 's a story in it,

And let me get at least a quarter through one

Before the feller comes out with a new one ;

And I 'd enjoy, once more, a poet's flutin'

That warn't all zigzag, friskin', hifalutin'.

Leave papers with some readin'-matter in

Betwixt the murders and patent medercin',

A room I dare set down in if a-faintin',

Some dinner-plates for puddin'—not for paintin';

A doctor not so swamped in his M. D.

His stuff ain't wuth a pinch of raspberry tea.

And let me mention, lest I be forgettin',

Leave me at least one good old hen for settin':

Them han'-made hens may hatch, but, for all
    weathers,

I 'll stick to an old speckled hen with feathers.

Well, this will do ; with these I 'll get along

The few days left.   If I have spoke too strong,

This mighty age—it must be mighty kind,

And pardin me for freein' of my mind.

www.ingramcontent.com/pod-product-compliance
Lightning Source LLC
Chambersburg PA
CBHW030104030726
47498CB00007B/2239